A HAIR SALON TO DIE FOR

A WONDERLAND BOOKS COZY MYSTERY
BOOK SIX

M.P. BLACK

"If you have built castles in the air, your work need not be lost; that is where they should be. Now put the foundations under them." — *Henry David Thoreau*

For A., without whose support, my castles would remain in the air. — *M.P.*

CHAPTER 1

*A*s Alice and Ona came into Candy's Hair Salon, Becca looked at them in the mirror. Her eyes danced with panic. Why was Becca, who was usually such a rock, begging for help?

Candy tugged at Becca's big, curly mane of hair as if she were pulling the frayed threads of an old coat.

"Let's give these curls some freedom," she said, talking to Becca in the mirror. "Bring out the passion in you. You said yourself you wanted a change, didn't you?"

"I did..." Becca said.

"Well, then. Let's cut this way down. Give it some pixie sass. Then color it red."

"Red?" Ona said, stepping closer. Her one visible eye narrowed, her rhinestone-studded eyepatch glittering in the bright lights of the salon. "Red?"

Candy looked up. Alice guessed she was in her 50s. Her bright turquoise mascara complemented her permed hair, which was dyed a bright yellow, and her orange, tanning-bed skin. Her fake nails were a matching turquoise.

"Ladies," she said, stepping back from Becca. "Welcome to Candy's."

This was her salon. Four leather chairs, four mirrors, and a shelf for each with the tools of the trade: scissors, combs, brushes, and hair products, plus copies of tabloids and fashion magazines. All four hair stylists tended to customers this morning, and there was a cacophony of sounds—a hair dryer blowing, customers chatting, and music thumping from overhead speakers.

Candy picked up a folder with laminated pages, each one with a glossy photo showcasing a haircut. The models—not to mention their haircuts—reminded Alice of celebrity photos from a couple of decades ago, maybe more.

"Becca and I agreed this is her new look," Candy said.

Alice looked at the photo and bit back a gasp. The woman in the photo had curls, just like Becca, but that's where the similarity ended. In contrast to Becca's big, generous mane of hair, the model had short, stingy curls in a fiery red that could only come from dye. On a different person, it might be bold and beautiful, but on Becca—with her beautiful, natural hair...?

"Short," Candy confirmed. "And red."

"Candy," Ona said, glancing at Alice and giving her a meaningful look. "Got a minute? Come with me..."

Ona put an arm around Candy's shoulders, turning her away from Becca while telling her all about the lottery tickets on sale—the reason Alice and Ona were going door-to-door this morning.

With Candy gone, Becca's shoulders sank and she let out a breath of air. Alice moved close and took Becca's hand.

"Are you all right?" Alice whispered.

"Get me out of this."

"You want this haircut?"

Becca shook her head and then looked away.

Alice raised an eyebrow. "But...?"

"But I kinda agreed to Candy's suggestion, because my usual haircut is a trim, and it hardly costs a thing, and—" She glanced over at Candy. Ona was still pitching the lottery tickets. "—well, Candy needs the business."

This was classic Becca. If it meant helping a friend, she'd sacrifice her own wishes. Now she wouldn't want to go back on her promise to Candy, because it wasn't about the haircut —it was about supporting someone in the community.

Alice frowned, looking at herself in the mirror. She would never agree to Candy cutting her hair to pixie length and then dyeing it to support a local business. No, she'd do it because she wanted that look. She ran a hand through her hair and her fingers got caught in a tangle. When was the last time she'd had a haircut?

She turned toward Ona, only to find that Ona had gathered the stylists and other customers in a circle near the back, so she could pitch the Blithedale Future Fund Lottery to them all.

Mr. and Mrs. Oriel, a couple who'd retired to Blithedale recently, and whose matching glasses and clothes made them look like twins, were sitting in salon chairs next to each other. No doubt getting the same haircut.

"We don't gamble," Mrs. Oriel said.

"Except in Vegas," Mr. Oriel added.

"Of course," his wife agreed. "Except in Vegas."

"But this is different."

"Completely different."

Mr. Oriel frowned. "It is different, isn't it?"

"It is different," Ona said. "In this lottery, everyone wins. Here's how it works: any town resident can buy a ticket, whether or not you own a business in Blithedale. The winner gets to pick which business the Blithedale Future Fund invests the prize money in. Of course, it has to be a business in town that's not already received support from the fund. You can even pick your own business if you hold the winning number."

"What a wonderful idea," Mrs. Oriel said.

"And you can't call that 'gambling,'" Mr. Oriel said.

"No, in fact, it's more like charity."

Mr. Oriel nodded, digging under his salon cape and bringing out his wallet. "What a great way to help our town thrive. We'll buy two tickets."

The stylists showed an interest, too. There was Opal, a young woman with purple highlights in her raven-black hair; Nelson, a quiet guy with glasses, bowtie, and a fade to his well-styled Afro; and Sasha, whose punk hairdo, tattoos, and many piercings reminded Alice of Lisbeth Salander—the so-called Girl with the Dragon Tattoo from Stieg Larsson's *Millennium* crime novels.

Everyone dug out money to pay Ona, and Ona handed out lottery tickets.

After getting their tickets, Opal cried out, "Selfie!"

She threw her arms around Candy and Sasha, pulling them close and then holding out her phone to snap a photo.

Nelson hung back, staying out of the photo. He hadn't bought a ticket either. But then, as far as Alice could remember, he didn't live in Blithedale.

Sasha held up her ticket. "Oh, wow, my lucky number. Maybe it's a sign."

Opal looked at her own ticket and grimaced. "Double thirteen? Double bad luck. Typical…"

"You never know, Opal," Candy said, putting a comforting arm around the young woman's shoulders.

"Besides," Sasha said. "In this lottery, everyone wins."

"Yeah, whatever," Opal mumbled.

Candy clapped her hands. "All right, let's get back to work…"

Next to Alice, Becca tensed. Alice put a hand on her shoulder.

"Don't worry," she said. "I've got an idea…"

Candy returned to Becca's side, ready to trim off most of Becca's mane and then dye it red. She picked up a pair of scissors.

Alice said, "I think Becca would like a trim this time. Nothing fancy. Just the usual."

Candy's eyes widened. "Oh."

"Well, I—" Becca said.

Before Becca could reiterate her promise, Alice cut in, "But I'd like a haircut, too, so how about we book a time for me. Then you get a new customer."

"Sounds great," Candy said, smiling.

They looked at a calendar on a tablet and found a time the next morning that worked.

Becca looked at Alice in the mirror. She mouthed the words, "thank you."

A screech outside made Alice tense and turn around.

A crowd started chanting. An icy feeling ran down her neck. Were they really saying…?

"Kill, kill, kill…!"

CHAPTER 2

*A*cross the street from Candy's, a crowd had gathered, and they were chanting, "Kill, kill, kill…"

They clustered by the entrance in the wire fence that ringed the empty lot where Townsend Development once stood. Signs attached to the fence notified the public of a new building project, and beyond the open gate stood a bulldozer, a digger, and a shed.

Outside the construction zone, a man with a megaphone got up on a box and faced the crowd. The megaphone screeched again. That was what had startled Alice the first time she heard it.

Alice and Ona stood on the steps to Candy's.

"This project will kill the Blithedale Woods," the man with the megaphone said.

The crowd booed.

"But we won't allow it."

They cheered.

"We'll kill it!" he shouted.

"Kill, kill, kill…" they chanted.

Alice recognized the man. His name was Silas, and he ran the Blithedale Woods Conservation Society.

Silas continued to talk into the megaphone, demanding the building project stop. The crowd chanted. Alice recognized some of them: Andrea from the cafe next door, Bonsai & Pie; Lorraine, the public librarian, and Lorraine's best friend, Sandy, tall as a redwood tree; Kendra Digby, owner of the Mystic Tree new age shop; as well as Fran, who, if Alice wasn't mistaken, had once worked at Candy's.

Ona said, "Silas sure knows how to inspire people."

"No denying it," Alice said.

"But can he really stop the new building project?"

"I don't know," Alice said. "I don't even know why he should. It seems crazy to leave that empty lot open on Main Street—it's prime real estate."

Ona nodded.

Mr. and Mrs. Oriel passed them, heading home, pleased with their new haircuts. Opal, escorting them out, crossed her arms. She said, "Those protesters are going to make us look bad."

"Oh, I wouldn't worry so much," Candy said behind her, apparently also curious. "It's got nothing to do with us."

Sasha, leather jacket and purse over her shoulder, stepped past them. "It's got everything to do with us. What would our town be without the woods?"

At that moment, a massive motorbike roared up Main Street, pulling over to the curb near the protesters. Its driver looked as big as a gorilla, his muscles straining the leather jacket he wore. He turned to the hair salon and waved.

"Babe!"

Sasha, a big smile on her face, waved back.

"Cliff's here," she said. "See you all later."

She dashed across the street.

"Have fun," Opal said with high-pitched cheerfulness. As

soon as Sasha was gone, however, Opal's face fell into a frown.

Nothing sincere about that cheerfulness, Alice thought.

Sasha's boyfriend, Cliff, was parking his bike. She threw her arms around him and he gave her a kiss. Then the two of them, holding hands, wandered over to join Silas and the protesters.

"Sasha thinks she's such a saint," Opal muttered.

"She cares about our town," Candy said. "That's a good thing."

"*Our* town? She's lived in Blithedale for a couple of years. She can't call it hers yet."

Alice studied Opal's frowning face. It could take a long time for outsiders to be accepted in a small town like Blithedale. But sometimes people used old prejudices to justify fresh resentment. Despite what she'd said, Opal's disapproval probably wasn't about how long Sasha had lived in Blithedale. Maybe the two simply didn't get along.

Candy said, "It's a good thing that someone like Sasha moves to town. We need fresh ideas, fresh blood, don't we?"

"Fresh blood," Opal said and snorted. "You call that punk look 'fresh'?"

Opal turned away from the drama across the street and headed back to her station. She plonked down on her chair, brought out her smartphone, and began scrolling. Behind her, Nelson was trimming his customer's neck hair, apparently entirely focused on his work.

"Well, back to work," Candy said with a shrug. "See you tomorrow morning, Alice."

The door to Candy's shut and Alice and Ona crossed the street, both curious about the protest. They weren't the only ones curious. People had stopped on their way down Main Street to gawk. And among them stood Mayor MacDonald, leaning against his SUV, his arms crossed on his chest.

Silas had finished his speech. He was talking to some of his fellow protesters.

A woman approached Alice and Ona. It was Fran, the hairstylist who used to work at Candy's. She had short, dark hair. Shadows darkened her eyes, as if she hadn't been getting enough sleep.

"I hear you're selling lottery tickets," she said.

Ona explained the concept to Fran, and how the Blithedale Future Fund, which usually supported local business through loans, was funding the lottery as a special "random" gift to the community.

"That's a wonderful idea," Fran said. "I'll buy a ticket."

"Hold on, Fran," Silas said, pushing through the crowd to get to them.

Silas was in his 40s, but he had a youthful energy about him that made him seem younger than some of his contemporaries.

He put a hand on Fran's shoulder, restraining her. "Don't buy a lottery ticket, Fran."

Fran gave him an uncertain look, then stepped back from Ona, yielding to his demand. Alice frowned. She didn't like how Silas had stepped in and told Fran what to do.

Then he turned around, ensuring people around him were paying attention. He raised his voice. "In fact, no one should buy any more tickets until they make the rules fair."

Alice said, "Oh? And what do you consider 'fair,' Silas?"

"The fund—and this lottery—only supports for-profit businesses. If you want our town to truly thrive, you need to invest in nonprofits, too."

"Like your conservation society?"

"Yes, like my conservation society." Silas corrected himself: "*Our* conservation society."

"Well, that's just—"

9

Alice was about to say, "Self-serving." But Ona gave her a hard nudge, and she stopped herself.

Ona said, "That's a good point, Silas. We'll consider it."

"Good. Until you change the rules, however, I can't endorse this lottery."

Endorse?

Alice clenched her fists. Who did he think he was?

"Endorse?" a voice said. "Who do you think you are?"

It was Mayor MacDonald. He must've heard the conversation, because now he pushed his way through the crowd, heading toward Silas.

Mayor MacDonald could've won a Mark Twain-lookalike competition. He had the same mustache, unruly hair, and white suit that Alice associated with the famous author. He smiled at Alice, pointedly ignoring Ona, because of their old feud, and then gave Silas a nasty look.

"Did I hear you meddling in the Blithedale Future Fund's new lottery? Just like you've been meddling with my building project."

"I'm here to ensure Blithedale—and its woods—can thrive."

"You're here to ensure we retreat to the Dark Ages by driving people and businesses away from our town."

Silas crossed his arms, his jaw setting. "And you'd prefer to bulldoze the woods so you can make more money off real estate. It's all about me, me, me, isn't it?"

"How dare you?" Mayor MacDonald's face flushed. "I've done more for this town's growth than anyone."

Silas snorted. "Please…"

Ona said, "Boys, boys, please calm down."

The two men ignored her. Mayor MacDonald stuck out a finger and with every sentence, poked Silas in the chest.

"You." Poke. "Know." Poke. "Nothing." Poke. "About—"

Silas shoved the mayor's hand away. "Touch me again, and I'll—"

Mayor MacDonald poked Silas again. "You'll what?"

Silas swung back an arm, as if to punch the mayor.

"Enough."

Alice pushed in between the two men, driving them apart. Ona grabbed Silas by the shoulders and turned him around, while Alice gripped Mayor MacDonald's arm and hauled him off, too. The mayor said, "Ouch," but Alice ignored him, leading him away.

"Typical that you two would side with Silas," Mayor MacDonald grumbled.

"We're not siding with anyone. We're trying to keep you two children from coming to blows."

The mayor turned on her. That finger shot up again.

If he pokes me, Alice thought, frowning at his finger, *I might be the one to start a fistfight.*

But he only stabbed at the air.

"I'm right," he insisted. "You'll see. I've made this town what it is—and I'll keep fighting for what's right, even if everyone of you fights me."

Then he spun around, strode around his SUV, and got into the driver's seat.

He revved the engine. The big black car roared down the street.

CHAPTER 3

*A*fter another hour of going door-to-door with Ona and selling more lottery tickets, Alice returned to Wonderland Books. Inside, it was quiet and cozy. The tiny house bookstore looked like a miniature log cabin, complete with exposed beams and rough-hewn wooden floorboards. Built-in shelves dominated the 400-square-foot space, each inch crammed with books.

On the counter lay a copy of *Walden* by Thoreau. She picked it up, flipping through the pages. It was a used copy someone had donated to Wonderland, and the previous owner had underlined passages here and there.

Thoreau wrote that "books are the treasured wealth of the world and the fit inheritance of generations and nations." She couldn't agree more. And this: "Things do not change; we change."

She could relate. When her mom got cancer, it had uprooted her from Blithedale. She'd been only 9 years old. Then her mom died and everything changed. Or, in some ways, nothing changed: she moved from place to place with her aunt and uncle, never settling down to become the person she ought to be. Twenty years later, she came back to Blithedale looking for a part of herself she'd left behind, buried deep down inside. She found it. Although two decades had brought change to Blithedale, the real transformation happened within her.

She opened the store for the day and turned her attention to restocking shelves and rearranging the display tables with books. One of them had a sign that said, "Nature." A pile of *Walden* paperbacks sat next to Annie Dillard's *Pilgrim at Tinker Creek*. She also had copies of Rachel Carson's *Silent Spring* and Bill McKibben's *The End of Nature*.

As she was considering the books, a customer stepped through the doorway. She turned to see if she could be helpful and found herself staring at Mayor MacDonald's frowning face. He wasn't looking at her. He was looking at her book display.

"What's this?" he asked.

"Books."

"Did Silas put you up to this?"

Alice sighed. "No one 'put me up to this.' This is my display of books on nature."

"I came to talk to you about the lottery—"

"Oh?"

"—to urge you to stick to your guns, and not change the rules. Just so Silas can get more money for his pet projects. I know Ona won't listen to reason. But now I can see I've been a fool to believe you'd be impartial."

"Excuse me? What are you talking about?"

Mayor MacDonald picked up the Bill McKibben book and then immediately let it drop, as if it were toxic. "This is what I'm talking about. You've jumped on Silas's bandwagon. You're supporting his propaganda campaign by selling these kinds of books."

"That's ridiculous," Alice said. "I've always had a display

table of nature books. Tourists come to Blithedale because of nature."

"Ah, here it comes," Mayor MacDonald said, making an impatient gesture with his hand.

"Here comes what?"

"You're about to give me a lecture on how nature is key to the town's future."

"Well, isn't it? If beautiful nature didn't surround us, people wouldn't visit, people wouldn't move here—and where would your real estate business be then?"

Mayor MacDonald's face turned red. "Don't lecture me on my business."

Alice laughed. "Then don't lecture me on mine."

She studied him. He glanced left and right. He crossed his arms, then fidgeted with his suit, smoothing it out. Then crossed his arms again. She'd never seen him so anxious.

"Mayor MacDonald, what is going on? Is this new development project stressing you out?"

"I don't get stressed out," he grumbled. "I get invested in things."

"All right. Then how *invested* are you?"

A twitch appeared under his right eye. "None of your business."

Wow, Alice thought. *He's really stressed. He must've invested a lot of money with the development company that's building the new project across from Candy's.*

Mayor MacDonald, besides serving as mayor, ran MacDonald Realty, the town's only realtor.

"You don't usually invest in development projects, do you?"

"I've dabbled before," he said.

"But nothing this big, huh?" She put a hand on his arm. "It's normal to feel overwhelmed. I mean, when I started this bookstore—"

He tore his arm free. "Don't belittle me," he snapped. "This is a major real estate project. A new office building for Blithedale that'll attract new corporate interests. This isn't some little bookshop in a tiny house."

Alice's insides clenched. Pressure was building inside her. She crossed her arms, trying to keep it in. "Well, excuse me for trying to empathize."

Mayor MacDonald snorted. "I don't need your pity. What I need is for you to stop pandering to these conservation nuts. As a member of the Blithedale Future Fund, you have a responsibility to this town."

The pressure increased. She gritted her teeth.

Don't lecture me about my responsibilities...

Before Alice could speak her angry words, Mayor MacDonald turned around and headed to the door. But he stopped in the doorway and looked back.

"A word of advice, Alice," he said. "You women can't always see the truth, but Silas is trouble—and if he keeps stoking up hatred, someone is going to get hurt."

"'You women'?"

The anger that she'd been holding back burst up from her gut and into her chest, and from there pulsed into her limbs. She wanted to roar with anger.

You women? How dare he...?

Mayor MacDonald strode out, slamming the door behind him.

Alice grabbed her copy of *Walden* off the counter and threw it at the door.

Thunk. It fell to the floor.

CHAPTER 4

That night, Alice met Becca and Ona at the Woodlander Bar for a much-needed drink.

"What is going on with Mayor MacDonald?" Alice asked. "He's so, so—"

"Ornery?" Ona suggested, then shrugged. "Nothing new about that."

"You and the mayor have never gotten along," Becca said. Then frowned. "But Alice is right: he's behaving terribly. It's not like him."

"He's in over his head in this development project," Alice said. "The man's a realtor, not an investor in development projects, and I think the stress is getting to him. But his rudeness…"

"Imagine how bad it will get when he hears we changed the lottery rules?" Ona said.

"He'll get over it," Becca said. "And then he'll return to his usual cheerful self."

Alice couldn't remember when she'd last seen the man smile. These days, the mayor's face carried a constant scowl, and his temper was a ticking time bomb, ready to explode at any moment. But nothing excused his comments.

She took a deep breath, the anger from earlier in the day still roiling in her gut. There was more to this problem than rudeness, though.

She said, "Acting as mayor while running a realty business was already a conflict of interest. But this new development project makes me wonder about his motives."

Ona laughed. "His motives have always been crystal clear: he wants to make money. The more, the merrier."

"That's not fair..." Becca said, and launched into a defense of Mayor MacDonald, who she'd known her entire life.

Alice sipped her drink, only half-listening to Becca. She was drinking a hard-liquor lemonade in a mason jar with fresh lemon and a sprig of thyme. The Woodlander Bar, a tiny house sitting in a clearing in the woods, served as the town's only bar. Ona had built the tiny house, but it was the bartender, Thor, who kept people coming back again and again for the incredible cocktails. Recently, a restaurant, Under the Greenwood Tree, had joined the bar, allowing customers to sit outside and eat dinner while also enjoying high-quality drinks.

Alice scanned the familiar faces. Many of the tables in the area between the two tiny houses—the restaurant and the bar—were occupied. As she studied the crowd, two people approached their table. She recognized them from Candy's Hair Salon.

Sasha gave them a big smile. Behind her, Nelson hung back.

"Great news about the lottery," Sasha said. "I heard you changed the rules to let people donate to the conservation society."

Ona nodded. "And any other nonprofit based in Blithedale."

"Well, I know which one I'll donate to if I win. The conservation society is doing incredible work. Any chance I've got, I support them." She smiled. "I mean *us*. I'm pretty involved in the organization."

"Good for you," Ona said, and Alice thought her friend really meant it. "We'll announce the winning number on *The Blithedale Record*'s site at midnight. So, tomorrow, we'll all know who the winner is."

"I'm excited," Sasha said. "I've got a good feeling about this."

As Sasha and Nelson found a table near the bar, Alice reflected on the decision the three of them had made to change the lottery rules.

"In the end, Silas got what he wanted," she said. "It seems he always does."

Ona nodded. "He's got a way with words. But, to be fair, he was right. The Blithedale Future Fund's mission is to invest in this town's future. How can we do that without investing in nonprofits, too?"

They'd gone over this earlier in the day, debating the pros and cons. In the end, the three of them—Alice, Becca, and Ona—had agreed that it was a major oversight on their part to limit the fund's support to for-profits. Alice felt good about the decision to change the lottery rules, but she couldn't help but feel defensive about it—no doubt because Mayor MacDonald's accusation still echoed in her mind.

I've got no reason to be defensive, she told herself. *I'm not on Silas's bandwagon.*

Just then, she caught sight of Silas in the parking lot. He was emerging from a car. Fran jumped out from the passenger side. Something about the way they behaved around each other...it almost seemed as if they were a couple.

Almost, Alice thought. *But not quite.*

She couldn't explain why, but something about how Silas moved a few feet ahead of Fran, and how she followed, made her think the relationship wasn't so straightforward.

Silas strode over to where Sasha and Nelson were sitting. Silas talked, Sasha grinned, and Nelson made some excuse—at this distance, Alice couldn't hear—and got up and hurried inside the tiny house to the bar.

Ona broke Alice's concentration by saying, "Another round?"

"I'll get more drinks," Alice said quickly, curious to get close to Silas, Sasha, and Fran, and maybe overhear what they were saying.

She gathered up the empty glasses and headed for the bar. As she passed the other table, Fran was talking, but Sasha interrupted.

"I know Nelson feels the same way," she told Fran. "The answer is still no."

"How can I change your mind?" Fran asked.

"I'm not interested right now. I'm better off focusing my energies on the conservation society. We've got a lot of work to do there."

Silas cut in. "Hold on a minute, Sasha. What do you mean by that?"

Alice couldn't linger without looking like she was eavesdropping, so she stepped through the doorway to the bar. At the counter, Nelson turned around with two drinks in mason jars, one for him and one for Sasha. Alice smiled as they passed, and Nelson looked away.

Not exactly Mr. Sociable, Alice thought.

At the bar, Thor looked as handsome as ever in a blue shirt that accentuated his blue eyes. His long blonde hair fell over one shoulder in a ponytail. His face broke into a broad smile when he saw her.

"What can I get you, Alice?"

She ordered another round. As he made the drinks, she asked him whether he knew Nelson. He shook his head and said, "He's a quiet guy. Doesn't say much. I've only seen him twice here, both times with Sasha."

He handed Alice the drinks, and she carried them outside, careful not to trip and spill them. As she passed Sasha and Nelson's table again, Silas was standing, arms akimbo, over Sasha. He spoke in a commanding voice.

"Your money doesn't give you special influence."

"Silas, I never said that," Sasha said.

"Actions speak louder than words."

"Come on, be reasonable—"

"I've said what needed saying. Come on, Fran. We're leaving."

Silas spun around, and grabbing Fran by the arm, strode away, hauling his companion with him. She stumbled alongside him for a few paces, then caught her balance and hurried along with him. A moment later, they were in Silas's car again. The engine came to life.

Back at the table with Becca and Ona, Alice set down the drinks. They all looked toward the parking lot, where Silas's car pulled out and, engine revving, drove off. A moment later, it vanished around the bend in the road, obscured by the trees.

"Nothing like a little drama," Ona said.

"What was that about?" Becca asked.

Alice shrugged. "I'm guessing Sasha and Silas don't see eye to eye."

But she wondered about what Silas had said—something about Sasha's influence. Over Silas and the conservation society?

CHAPTER 5

*B*ecca drove back home in her candy apple red 1966 Ford Thunderbird convertible, while Alice hitched a ride in Ona's pickup truck. They were rumbling down Main Street, which was deserted at this time of night, when she saw a flash of light behind a window.

She turned and looked over her shoulder.

There it was again. It looked like a flashlight, its beam swinging across a window.

Not just any window.

"Isn't that Candy's salon back there?"

Ona looked in her rearview mirror. "Yup."

"Stop the truck, Ona. Someone's inside."

"Maybe Candy stopped by on her way home."

"And used a flashlight?"

They exchanged glances.

"Let's go take a look," Ona said.

Ona pulled over to the curb and parked. They got out and moved up Main Street. On their right, the construction zone for the new development project lay in shadowy darkness. To the left, the buildings were dark. Except there it was again: a beam of light flashing across the front windows of Candy's Hair Salon.

Alice and Ona strode across the street.

Through the glass, Alice could see a shadow move around.

"Burglar," Ona said and went to the door and banged on it. "Hey!"

The person inside froze. Then, before Alice could make out who it was, the burglar turned and bolted.

"They're getting out the back," Alice said.

She and Ona hurried around the building, heading down the narrow alley between the salon and the Bonsai & Pie cafe. But before they'd made it halfway to the back, a roar broke the silence of the night.

Alice stopped dead in her tracks, startled. So did Ona.

They looked at each other.

The roar repeated, and this time, Alice realized it was an engine revving. Up ahead, a shape flashed past the end of the alley and then turned. Alice ran forward, with Ona close behind her. As they emerged at the back, where the woods began, Alice saw the taillight of a motorbike as it sped up a trail.

"We'll never catch it," Ona said.

Ona was right. And a moment later, the bike was gone.

"At least we scared the burglar off," Ona said. "But we'd better call the cops."

Alice nodded, staring off into the dark woods.

Who would want to break into Candy's salon?

CHAPTER 6

*I*n the morning, Alice returned to Candy's Hair Salon. As she approached the salon, she saw two people standing outside by the door: Sasha and Opal.

"Morning," Alice greeted them.

"Are you here for a haircut?" Sasha asked. "I'll be your stylist today."

Sasha dug out a keychain from her pocket. It had a cute little lollipop charm attached to it. She unlocked the door and pushed it open, motioning for Alice to step inside. But before Alice could do so, Opal walked inside, apparently oblivious to her own rudeness.

Sasha gave Alice a look—a raised eyebrow—that suggested she knew all about Opal's rudeness.

Then she said, "Before we get started, I've got to look for my lottery ticket. I left it here yesterday." She grinned. "I've got a good feeling…"

Inside, Alice scanned the salon, looking for signs of a break-in. The four chairs facing the mirrors stood in a neat line. The equipment on the shelves appeared undisturbed, at least as far as Alice could tell.

Sasha, who'd gone to the back, returned. She bent over a drawer and rummaged in its contents.

Alice said, "I know there was a break-in last night. But it doesn't look like the burglar made much of a mess."

Sasha looked up. She glanced around. "You're right. Anyway, I'm sure Candy will learn more once she's talked to the cops again. She called me early this morning and asked me to open up, since she'd be in Tilbury Town visiting the county sheriff and then finding a locksmith."

She bent over the drawer again, digging among the items.

Alice said, "The burglar didn't bust the front door lock, did they?"

"No. The back door looks OK, too. Maybe Candy wants better, more secure locks. Anyway, the burglar must've figured out how to switch off the alarm system."

"It's broken?"

"Oh, no, it's just off."

"And Opal didn't switch it off?"

Opal was sitting in the chair at her station, leaning close to the mirror while touching up her makeup. She said, "No, I didn't switch it off. How would I? I don't know the code."

Sasha, now rummaging in a different drawer, said, "She's right. I don't know the code, either. Usually, Candy shows up early and opens the salon."

Alice glanced over at Opal, who was done with her makeup. She was taking selfies of herself, then hunching over her phone, apparently selecting the best shot and posting it to social media.

Sasha let out a huff of frustration and straightened up.

"Where did I put that lottery ticket...?" Then noticed Alice. "Sorry, I'm totally neglecting you. Come on over to the sinks." She handed Alice a cape to wear. "We'll start by shampooing your hair."

Alice settled into the reclining shampoo chair. Sasha

began washing her hair in warm water and massaging her scalp. It felt nice to be pampered. Alice closed her eyes, relishing the warm water and Sasha's hands in her wet hair.

"All done," Sasha said, and Alice, feeling sleepy, reluctantly opened her eyes.

Another couple of minutes of that and she would've been snoring.

Sasha led her to one of the leather-and-steel chairs by a mirror, saying, as Alice sat down, "All right, so what do you want to do?"

Alice thought of what Candy wanted to do to Becca's hair and shuddered. "Just a trim, please. Nothing radical."

If one word described Sasha's style—piercings, tattoo, and jagged haircut—it must be "radical." But she didn't push Alice. She simply smiled and said, "Great. You have nice hair. No need to do much."

"Yes!" Sasha exclaimed. She leaned forward and picked something up from the shelf by the mirror. "Here it is," she said, and stared at the ticket. "What was the winning number?"

Alice dug out her phone and read the number from *The Blithedale Record*'s announcement. As far as Alice knew, the winner hadn't stepped forward yet. Could it be Sasha?

"The winning number is 7017," she said.

"Oh." Sasha's face fell. She crumpled the ticket and threw it on the shelf.

"Better hold on to that," Alice said. "The winner hasn't stepped forward yet, and if the person doesn't claim the prize, then we may need to pull a second number."

"Good point." She picked up the ticket and put it in her pocket. She took a deep breath and then let it out. "Now, let's do something about your hair, huh?"

She bent down, rummaging underneath the main shelf by the mirror.

"Hey, Opal, where's my hairdryer?"

"How should I know?"

"You borrowed it yesterday."

"And I put it back."

Sasha gestured toward Opal. "Like you put your other things back."

There was a jar of something on the shelf in front of Opal. Opal flicked it with a finger. On the side it said, in large orange letters, "Mochaccino Mix."

"OK, so maybe I forgot to put this back, but I definitely returned your blow dryer."

"Well, it's not here. And where are my scissors?"

"Take Nelson's."

Sasha sighed. She went to another station and got a blow dryer and a pair of scissors. Alice wondered about the missing things.

"Sasha, do you think the burglar stole your blow dryer and scissors?"

"Why would a burglar steal one blow dryer and one pair of scissors?" Lowering her voice, she said, "More likely, Miss Selfie over there misplaced them."

"I heard that," Opal said. "Anyway, who wants a mochaccino?"

Looking at Alice in the mirror, Sasha said, "Opal makes these mochaccinos with whipped cream and chocolate syrup. They're pretty decadent. And then she doesn't even drink them."

"You don't drink them?" Alice asked Opal.

"They're part of my personal brand. But I don't want the calories."

Sasha said, "Opal's trying to be an influencer on social media."

"Not 'trying to be,'" Opal said, getting up from her chair.

"I am an influencer. And last chance: do you both want a mochaccino?"

Alice eyed the jar with the mochaccino mix dubiously. She didn't like sweet coffee drinks. A latte was fine, but once the coffee was mixed with cocoa powder, overpowered by syrup, and buried in whipped cream, she couldn't see the point.

She shook her head. "No, thanks."

"You, Sasha? Oh, come on, I know you can't resist my mochaccino."

Sasha laughed. "Guilty as charged. I'm the only one with a big enough sweet tooth for that stuff."

Opal grabbed the jar and headed into the back of the salon. As Sasha got started on her hair, Alice could hear Opal out back clattering around. There was the rumbling sound of an espresso machine at work, then the pfft of a can of whipped cream dispensing its contents.

A moment later, Opal emerged from the back with a coffee mug overflowing with whipped cream and decorated with a swirl of chocolate syrup.

She had to hand it to Opal. Even if Alice wouldn't like the taste, it looked beautiful.

Sasha reached for the mug, but Opal held on to it.

"Photo first," she said, and Sasha sighed.

"Always photo first."

"Always."

Opal positioned herself next to Sasha. They leaned close and Opal held up the mug of mochaccino in one hand and her phone in the other, snapping several selfies. After she was done, she handed Sasha the coffee drink.

Sasha took a sip and licked the whipped cream off her upper lip.

"The mochaccino is just a photo op," Sasha explained.

"Not 'just' anything," Opal protested. "It's an example of

my *amazing* generosity toward my friends, which my online followers *love*."

In the mirror, Alice caught Sasha rolling her eyes. But she took another sip of the coffee drink. She licked her lips again and said, "Opal, you must've used less mix than usual. It's usually sweeter."

"Can't get much sweeter," Opal said.

"You try it," Sasha said, holding out the mug. "It's bitter."

"No, thanks. And if you don't like it, you don't have to drink it. I got my selfie."

But as Sasha worked on Alice's hair, she continued to drink the mochaccino, occasionally wincing, as if the bitterness got worse once she'd eaten the whipped cream on top. She got more animated as she snipped the hair. In fact, she moved faster and faster—to the point where Alice worried about how close those scissors were coming to her ears.

But Sasha seemed oblivious. She was busy talking a million miles a minute, only rarely pausing to breathe. "And then I got this idea and told Silas that the conservation society should expand its range but he said no way and that's fine because I can set up something myself with or without his help and that's something he wasn't so happy about, so anyway, I'd need funding and I thought the lottery money could get me what I needed and I felt so sure I would win but I didn't and—"

She took another sip of her drink.

The door opened and Candy stepped inside with a cheerful, "Hello, everyone. I'm back." She was grinning. "And guess what happened? I got the number. I won the lottery!"

"That's amazing," Alice said. "Congratulations."

"Yeah, awesome," Opal said from behind her phone. "I knew my number was a dud."

Sasha didn't react to the news. She was leaning against

Alice's chair. She ran a hand across her forehead. "Is it hot in here? I feel hot. It's hot. Do you feel hot?"

Alice shook her head. "I'm fine. But, Sasha, are you all right? You look flushed."

"It's just hot, and I feel—" She shook herself. "I feel—"

She stopped talking. Her eyes went wide as she shook.

No, Alice realized, she wasn't shaking. She was convulsing.

The scissors fell to the floor with a clatter.

"Sasha?"

"Sasha, what's wrong?" Candy said.

Sasha's eyes rolled back in her head. Her teeth chattered. She doubled over, as if her stomach seized up, and she let out a sound like a choked groan: "Gaaaaaaaahhh…"

"Sasha!"

Then Sasha fell.

And she didn't get back up.

CHAPTER 7

That evening, Alice sat in the lounge at the Pemberley Inn, cradling a large mug of tea in her hands. Ona sat next to her. Across from her sat Captain Walt Burlap of the State Police Bureau of Investigation. A wide-shouldered man in his 40s, Captain Burlap wore his strength with calm confidence. Alice thought of him as a kind of gentle giant, and she was grateful the chief police investigator was a gentle giant. Right now, her nerves couldn't handle anyone brash.

Burlap stroked his thick stubble as he talked.

"...and so we'll have to wait for the final forensics report, but the county coroner's pretty sure we're dealing with a case of poisoning. He believes it was cocaine. Given how quickly the victim deteriorated, I'd say the dose must've been massive. There was nothing you could do."

Alice, feeling numb, nodded. She'd tried to revive Sasha, applying first aid while Opal called emergency services. But without luck. Sasha was gone.

"I've got questions," Burlap said.

Alice did, too. But her whole body felt stiff, her mind

numb, and the questions wouldn't form into coherent sentences. Though one kept repeating over and over in her mind: why?

She said, "I thought I already answered your questions back at the diner."

"You did," he agreed. "And I've got more than enough to write my official report, pending input from forensics, of course. But this isn't for my official report."

Alice had made her statement already. After the first responders arrived, the cops questioned Alice. Then, at the diner, Captain Burlap went over the events with her, from meeting Sasha and Opal at the door to Sasha's sudden, convulsive death. So his visit this evening came as a surprise.

When he arrived, she'd been sitting in the lounge with Ona, drinking cup after cup of warm tea to thaw her bones, even though the inn was warm and the spring evening mild. Truth be told, she was glad he'd come—it wasn't as if she could stop thinking about what happened, anyway.

She said, "If it's not for your official report, then how can I help?"

"You've been involved in murder cases before. I know you had a big hand in the former chief of police's successes."

Alice shrugged.

Burlap was referring to Chief Jimbo, who'd recently resigned, effectively shutting down the single-cop police department in Blithedale. Jimbo had been ill-suited to police work. He'd moved down to Florida to visit his dad while he figured out his next career move. Blithedale now relied on the state police and the county sheriff.

"Your silence is modesty," Burlap said. "I know how involved you've been, Alice—and you, too, Ona. And so I'm here, off the record, to ask about the stuff I can't put in my report."

"The good stuff?" Ona suggested.

Burlap smiled. "It's all good stuff, if you ask me."

"You mean my thoughts on Sasha's death?" Alice said.

"That's right. Your thoughts, impressions, and theories. Normally, I wouldn't ask this of someone who'd witnessed a death, especially since I should treat you as a potential suspect. Which is why this isn't going in my report. But I trust you—and I value your opinion." He smiled. "From one investigator to another."

His words warmed her. Despite how miserable she felt, she smiled back at him.

"I'll try to help. I'll do my best."

"I expected nothing less."

"But," she added, shaking her head, "I won't play detective. Those other times, I needed to get involved because Chief Jimbo wasn't pulling his weight. You say you trust me. Well, I trust you, too, and I don't see how my meddling will be a good thing."

"We can discuss the merits of your meddling some other time," Burlap said. "Right now, I'd appreciate your thoughts. What happened this morning? Forget the bare facts and tell me what you think."

Alice took a sip of tea, the horrific scene replaying in her head for the hundredth time.

"Someone poisoned Sasha. The killer knew she would drink Opal's mochaccino. Sasha herself said no one else drank the stuff. Which means someone could poison the mix and be fairly certain that Sasha would drink it." She thought for a moment. "Or a customer would. In fact, the killer ran a colossal risk."

Burlap nodded. "Yes, but Opal claims to never have served it to a customer. It was her own mix. She usually kept it in the break room. Candy never added mochaccino to the menu for customers, because, she says, it would take too long to prepare—it was a distraction."

"The killer must've known. Opal herself could've spiked the mix. Or anyone else passing through the salon."

"Except Opal made a mochaccino the afternoon before, and that didn't kill anyone. So what happened between yesterday afternoon and this morning?"

"The burglary."

"That's my theory, too. Whoever wanted to poison Sasha snuck in at night and tampered with the mochaccino mix."

"A person on a motorbike." Alice frowned. "I wish I could give you a clearer picture of who we saw at the salon last night."

Burlap nodded. "And unfortunately, the tire marks from the motorbike or dirt bike, or whatever it was, weren't clear enough to identify it. The ground was too hard and dry. Plus, the salon itself is a mess of fingerprints, and DNA traces won't do us much good, either." He leaned forward. "You've already made a statement about what happened and what Sasha said. But thinking back, what stood out to you?"

Alice considered his question. Before going into convulsions, Sasha became more and more agitated. She'd talked faster and faster, and she'd said so much, so quickly, that Alice found it difficult to remember every detail.

But there was one thing...

"Silas," she said. "She talked about how she'd wanted to change something about the conservation society and Silas hadn't liked it." Saying it out loud brought back another memory. "Oh, and the other night, I overheard them having a kind of confrontation at the Woodlander Bar."

She told Burlap about Sasha's interaction with Silas, and how Silas and Fran had walked away, clearly displeased. Burlap scratched his chin, looking thoughtful.

"Interesting..."

Alice yawned, trying unsuccessfully to hold it back.

"That's my cue." Burlap stood up. "Ladies, I appreciate

your time. You—" He gestured at Alice. "—ought to go to bed. Tomorrow, you can give all this more thought."

Alice shook her head. "No, thanks. I'll leave that to you."

But after she'd said goodbye to Captain Burlap and Ona, and she'd climbed the stairs to her room—the Colonel Brandon Suite—she found she couldn't stop her mind from spinning around that central question: why?

She brushed her teeth, washed her face, and got into her pajamas. Getting comfortable in her canopy bed, with a pillow at her back, she opened her copy of *Walden*.

> *I had this advantage, at least, in my mode of life, over those who were obliged to look abroad for amusement, to society and the theatre, that my life itself was become my amusement and never ceased to be novel. It was a drama of many scenes and without an end.*

Alice snorted to herself. Right now, she wished her own "mode of life," as Thoreau called it, had a little less amusement. It definitely felt like a drama with many scenes and without an end. She let out a long sigh. Then tried to read some more, but the words danced across the page, refusing to settle down.

Finally, she gave up, slipped a bookmark into the pages, and placed the paperback on her bedside table. She turned off the light, lay down, and stared up at the darkness.

The investigation is in good hands, she thought. *I can stop worrying about it.*

Of course, her mind wouldn't stop worrying about it. She'd watched a woman die in front of her—you didn't simply let that go.

She turned over in bed and clutched her pillow.

No matter how awful that was, I don't need to play a role in this. Burlap may want my opinion. Fine. But no one is asking me to get involved.

She closed her eyes.

Why?

She pressed her eyes shut, as if pressing harder would push her toward sleep.

It didn't work. She turned over in bed, readjusting the pillow under her head. Then sighed and tried to go to sleep again.

She tossed and turned for what felt like hours.

Then, just as she felt herself slipping off to sleep, an odd sensation crept over her body. Like she was trembling. No, it was the bed—the bed was trembling.

She opened her eyes. Sasha was lying next to her in bed, facing her. She gazed at Alice with a calm determination that suggested she felt no pain. Not now—not anymore. She was at peace.

Her mouth didn't move, but somehow Alice heard her voice in her head.

Why? Sasha asked.

"I don't know," Alice whispered.

Then who?

Alice shook her head.

Why, Sasha repeated. *And who?*

Alice brought a hand to her eyes and rubbed them. Her fingers came away wet with tears. She blinked. Her bed was empty. Sasha was gone, leaving only the familiar silence and darkness.

A bad dream, she told herself.

But even as sleep took hold of her—a deep, deep sleep this time—Alice told herself that she owed Sasha an answer to her questions.

Who.

And why.

CHAPTER 8

"There it is," Ona said, pointing through the trees. "Sasha's house."

A tiny house—one of Ona's—stood deep in the woods. Given Sasha's dragon-tattoo aesthetic, Alice had expected something grittier. Gothic stone. Blood-red banners. Spikes on the roof. But Sasha's tiny house had flower pots outside with geraniums. The house itself was painted lavender with white trim.

A motorbike stood parked next to the house.

"And look who's here," Alice said.

"Cliff."

This was lucky. Because after an early breakfast at the diner—at which Alice had told Becca and Ona about her intention to help Captain Burlap with his investigation—they'd speculated about who could be the killer. None of them had an idea, but as Becca pointed out, most killers knew the victim intimately—murders usually happened thanks to a partner or a relative. So, they'd agreed that they ought to talk to Cliff, and Ona suggested they also take a look at Sasha's place in the woods. Finding Cliff here was killing two birds with one stone.

"What do you know about Cliff?" Alice asked Ona.

Ona shrugged. "Big, beefy guy with lots of tattoos. He works as a security guard for Tilbury Services over in Tilbury Town, and he used to work as a bouncer at bars. Before that, I think he spent his time getting into fights and challenging the bouncers."

"You don't think he's dangerous, do you?"

"Alice, we're trying to catch a killer. You have to expect a little danger."

Alice grimaced. She appreciated Ona's courage, but she'd seen just how big Cliff was. He looked like he ate booksellers for breakfast. Or he might, if he was hungry enough. And guys who lifted weights, weren't they always hungry?

Ona nudged her. "Stop worrying. We're a couple of friendly neighbors who are dropping by to share our condolences and make sure he's doing all right."

Alice looked around. A motorbike could come down the dirt path that led past the tiny house, but they'd been forced to abandon Ona's pickup truck to hike into the woods. Now she realized how isolated this place was. And how far from anyone else they were.

"Ona, there are no neighbors."

"We're figurative neighbors. Anyway, I know Gussie who lives in number 18 down the path."

"You mean the houses actually have numbers out here?"

"Sure. USPS delivers here, too. This isn't the depths of the Amazon rainforest. Now, come on."

Ona took her hand and dragged her forward. Alice wasn't sure why she was so spooked. It must've been the dream last night—Sasha turning up in her bed like that—which had left her with permanent goosebumps.

They approached the tiny house. The front door had a lintel painted with cute little flowers and a heart carved into it with the house number at the center. Again, Alice peered through the trees, wondering just how far it was to this unseen neighbor, Gussie. Would Gussie hear them if they screamed?

The door swung open. Cliff didn't just fill the doorway, he exceeded it: his shoulders weren't visible in the opening and he had to stoop down and peek under the lintel to see who'd come to visit.

He frowned.

"Yeah?"

"We thought we'd pay you a friendly, neighborly visit," Ona said with a bright smile.

"You're not Gussie."

He began to close the door.

But Alice stepped forward and said, "Ona built this house for Sasha. And I was there, at Candy's salon, the morning she—"

She swallowed.

Cliff's face had transformed from a standoffish frown to something horrific, as wild-eyed as one of those Japanese Kabuki demon masks. Then it crumpled. His lower lip quivered, and he ran a giant hand across his face, hiding his emotion. He turned his back to them.

He said, his voice muffled by his hand, "You can come in."

The tiny house had a cozy little counter and stove, a two-person kitchen bar, and a living room area with a loveseat and a TV. Cliff slumped onto the loveseat, which, given his gargantuan body, served more as an armchair than a small couch. He put his head into his hands and his shoulders shook.

Alice approached him cautiously. She perched on the edge of the loveseat and gently placed a hand on one of his huge shoulders.

"I'm so sorry, Cliff," she said.

"She was so—" A sob interrupted him. "—so good to me."

Ona, in the kitchen, was looking through cupboards. She found a jar of instant coffee, frowned, and turned to Alice. Alice shook her head. It was probably fine, but the idea of any kind of powder or mix gave her the heebie-jeebies. Ona found a box of tea bags and Alice gave her a thumbs up.

While Ona put on a kettle to make tea, Alice comforted Cliff.

"Sounds like you and Sasha had something special. You must have so many happy memories to think back on."

Cliff nodded. "Always laughing." He dropped his hands and looked up at Alice. "She was always laughing. But you know, she could be serious, too. She was serious about her home in the woods. She was serious about us..."

His breathing hitched, and Alice feared another round of sobs were welling up, so she tried to turn the conversation back onto Sasha's love for nature.

"She loved the woods," she said. "She did a lot for the conservation society."

Cliff sniffled. "She was a good person. So dedicated. I told her that one day she would end up running the society. Though I guess Silas wouldn't like that." Cliff shook his head. "That guy Silas has a bad temper."

"Did he get mad at Sasha?"

"Sometimes. But Sasha didn't worry. She had a way of turning anger into peacefulness. Like she did with me. I used to be so angry. I used to get into fights. But once I met Sasha —and I spent time with her out here in the woods—I became a different person. More, you know, in touch with my inner nature."

Ona came over with cups of tea. Cliff accepted his tea with a nod of thanks. For a while, he blew steam off his cup, saying nothing, apparently lost in thought.

Finally, he said, "People looked at Sasha, and they thought they knew who she was, what kind of person she was, but they were wrong. Sasha taught me you could enjoy your tattoos and piercings or weightlifting or heavy metal music and still find your calm inner spirit. You could be your own self."

He looked over at Alice and Ona.

"I feel I can tell you these things. Like you understand."

Alice nodded. "We understand."

Cliff frowned. "The cops came by to question me, and I didn't tell them a thing, except where I was at the time of the —" His lower lip quivered and before the sobs could overtake him, he guzzled some tea. When he'd swallowed, he said, "I told them the facts, and that was it. But I feel I can talk to you about who Sasha really was."

"You loved her."

"Who wouldn't?" he said. Then, more fiercely, "Well, who?"

"I don't know. It's hard to imagine, but someone wanted to hurt her. Why do you think someone might've wanted to—?"

She didn't finish her sentence. Somehow the words "kill her" seemed too harsh—she worried it would put Cliff over the edge.

Cliff stared at his tea. "I don't know."

Alice said, "You mentioned Silas got angry with her…"

Cliff shook his head. "Silas didn't hide his anger. He's like me. He wouldn't poison a person. He'd hit them. No, it must've been someone sneaky."

Alice was struck by how astute Cliff's reasoning was. The killer wasn't the type to kill a person by running them over in a truck or shooting them. The killer had carefully poisoned Sasha.

"Sneaky…" Cliff repeated, a frown gathering on his face.

"It makes me think of that Nelson guy. He was always lurking around Sasha, always so quiet. I never trusted him."

"Her colleague? But why would Nelson want to hurt Sasha?"

"They met for drinks at the Woodlander Bar. It was Sasha's idea. She felt bad for him. But then the next time, it was Nelson who suggested it. He rarely said a peep, but after that night, Sasha told me, he seemed eager to talk to her. She used the word 'hungry.'"

"Maybe he was lonely."

"She told me he asked her a lot of questions—including about me. As if he didn't trust me. Or maybe he wanted to push me out of her life." Cliff nodded at his own conclusion. He grew so eager, the tea sloshed over the rim of his cup. But he didn't seem to notice. "Yeah, I bet that's it. He wanted me to disappear, so he could have Sasha to himself."

Maybe Cliff knew more than he was sharing, but Alice couldn't follow the leap in logic. "Wait, you think he was in love with her?"

"Of course he was. And when he realized he couldn't have her, he—"

"He killed her?"

Cliff clammed up. He put aside his teacup.

"Excuse me," he said. "I've got to run an errand..."

CHAPTER 9

*B*ack at the diner, Alice tried to call Nelson. But he didn't answer. She tried again and again, and then finally gave up.

"I can't reach him."

"I wouldn't worry," Ona said, sipping her second cup of coffee. "Cliff might have a crazy idea in his head about Nelson, but do you really think he's going to do something desperate?"

They looked at each other, both knowing the answer to the question, both worried.

Had they made a mistake to talk to Cliff? Captain Burlap's questions hadn't led him to the conclusion that Nelson might be the killer. Cliff's idea of a motive was half-baked, and there was nothing connecting Nelson to the burglary, either. She called Captain Burlap and explained.

"Don't worry, Alice," he said. "I'm on it. I'll find Nelson or Cliff—or both of them—and straighten this out."

After the call, Alice let out a sigh of relief. She took another sip of coffee. She needed to get to work. But how could she think about her books when there was a killer on the loose? She sighed. She had to. The books wouldn't sell themselves.

"Ona," she said, "I'd better—"

Becca slid into the booth, trapping Alice on the inside. "We've got company."

Candy sat down next to Ona, across from Becca and Alice.

"Hi, everyone," she said, her voice low and lifeless. Dark pouches under her eyes showed how little sleep she'd gotten, and her eyes were red—no doubt from crying.

"Oh, Candy," Becca said, arranging a coffee cup in front of her. "I'm so sorry. This must all be a nightmare for you."

"Poor Sasha..." Candy clenched her fists, clearly fighting back tears. "We should be celebrating now, not grieving... Sasha would've been so happy..."

Ona nodded. "She was a generous person, wasn't she?"

"Incredibly generous." Candy sighed. "I was already feeling strange about winning. Honestly, I never thought I had a chance. My luck's been terrible lately. Business has slowed down. Then Fran, who I honestly thought would one day take over my salon, left me. She walked out. It was such a shock. And since then, the problems have gotten worse. I'm behind on my mortgage payments, and the bank says—"

She cut herself off. Becca poured her a cup of coffee. With a shaking hand, Candy lifted the cup to her lips and took a sip.

"But winning the lottery," Alice said. "It changes everything, right?"

"It can't change what happened to Sasha..." Candy stared at her coffee. "And I feel I should donate the money to Silas's conservation society."

"What? Why?"

"Because that's what Sasha would've wanted to use the money for."

Becca put a hand on Candy's. "That's a beautiful gesture, but you said yourself that Sasha would've been happy for you. She cared for your salon. If she knew the financial problems you faced, wouldn't she want to help? Wouldn't she want you to use the prize money to save your business?"

"I suppose..."

"Don't worry about the conservation society," Alice said. "That's what the Blithedale Future Fund is here for. We're looking at each local business—and nonprofit—and assessing which may need help."

"But not every business gets picked," Candy said. "And who's to say when the conservation society will receive funding? It may be passed over for some other organization or business."

"Well, that's true..." Alice rubbed her neck, feeling awkward. Did Candy know that, in an earlier round, they'd looked at her salon but decided not to support it? The fund wasn't a multi-million-dollar foundation. It had to limit its investments to businesses that were considered priorities for the town.

"I know my business isn't a priority," Candy said, as if knowing what Alice was thinking. "And that's only right. But now that I've won the lottery, is it fair that I then make my salon the top priority? And how can I ignore the new rules you introduced and *not* give to the conservation society or some other nonprofit? Especially when that's what poor Sasha wanted?"

Alice bit her lip. She didn't have good answers to Candy's questions. She looked at Becca and Ona. Becca reached across the table and took Candy's hands.

"There is no shame in investing in your own business."

"But there is shame in withholding money from others who need it more."

"As Alice said, the fund is here to help others. And we'll

now also be looking at how we can support nonprofits, like the conservation society."

"That's all fine and well, but—"

"Candy, sweetie, let me finish. When you bought that lottery ticket, you contributed money to the fund—money that others will benefit from—and you also signed up to win the chance to assign funding to your own business. We may have changed the rules to include nonprofits, but that doesn't change why you originally bought a ticket."

Ona cut in. "Becca's right. Think back to when you bought the ticket. What did you imagine you would do if you won?"

Candy sighed. "I was thinking I'd invest the money in my business. We even talked about it at the salon—me, Opal, Sasha, and Nelson. They were all supportive. Well, at least Sasha was."

"It's OK to stick to your original intentions."

Candy stared down at her coffee cup, now almost empty. Then she looked up at Ona, then Becca, and finally Alice. "Do you all really think so?"

Alice nodded. "Absolutely. It was the whole point of the lottery. We can find another way to honor Sasha's life."

Candy played with the handle on the coffee cup, running a finger along its curve. The conflicting thoughts played out on her face: her eyes narrowing, then widening again, her brows furrowing and straightening. Tears glistening in her eyes.

She must be thinking of Sasha again, Alice thought. *Who can blame her?*

Finally, Candy sighed and pushed the coffee cup aside. She gave a single nod.

"All right," she said. "I'll do it."

CHAPTER 10

Fran's new salon lay on the north road to town. Alice and Ona got out of the pickup truck and headed for the entrance. A banner hung over the low building's entrance that said, "Grand Opening."

The interior suggested a modern salon, like the ones you saw in the city or at malls. Compared with Candy's, Fran had more chairs—eight, in total—and the space was larger and airier. The surfaces were all white and glass and steel and mirrors. Near the back stood a massive chrome espresso machine. A soundtrack of chill hip-hop beats played from speakers above.

Three young stylists were tending to customers. Surprised, Alice recognized a fourth: it was Opal. After taking a selfie with the client whose hair she'd just cut, she turned to Alice with a smile.

"Hey, you."

"You work at two salons?" Alice asked.

"Nah. Fran offered me a job, and I jumped at it. I mean, we'd already talked about it, but after what happened at Candy's, I was, like, give me the job *now*." She shrugged.

46

"Who knows how long Candy's will be closed by the police, and a girl's gotta eat, right? Plus, it didn't look good for my personal brand." She held up her phone. "And a girl's gotta think about her followers."

Does a girl, really? Alice thought, but she kept her thought to herself. *Sasha just died, and you're already turning your back on Candy?*

Fran emerged from the back, moving swiftly across the floor. She was the reason Alice and Ona had come. Her connection to Silas might be significant. That night at the Woodlander, she'd approached Sasha and Nelson, and Sasha had rebuffed her. Sasha had said she wanted to focus her energy on the conservation society. But what was it Sasha had said no to? If Alice remembered correctly, she'd also said no on Nelson's behalf. Could it have something to do with Fran's new salon?

"Opal," she said, sounding harried. "Clean up. You've got another guest coming in a minute."

"Yeah, yeah, Mom," Opal muttered.

Fran frowned. "Opal, please."

Opal sighed. She grabbed a mini brush and dustpan and swept hair off her station.

Alice and Ona said hello to Fran.

"Are you here to get a haircut?" she asked. She eyed Alice. "Sorry for saying so, but your haircut looks asymmetrical."

Alice grimaced. Fran was right. After all, Sasha hadn't finished the trim when she'd fallen to the floor. After some back and forth, Alice allowed herself to be led to a chair for a quick dry cut by Fran herself.

"We actually stopped by to take a look at the new place," Alice said, as Fran hurriedly snipped the uneven locks of hair. "And then we saw Opal was working here."

"That's right." Fran eyed her suspiciously in the mirror. "I offered Opal a job. What about it? Don't I have the right to offer people jobs? If they decide to take it or not, that's their choice."

"We're not questioning your right to hire people," Ona said, putting a hand on Fran's shoulder to calm her.

Fran pinched the bridge of her nose and squeezed her eyes shut. "Sorry, I've got a headache. And the awful news about Sasha…"

She went back to trimming Alice's hair, moving in with the scissors with a precision and expertise that was impressive to watch. One of the young stylists interrupted her with a question. Then she got back to working on Alice's hair.

Alice said, "Did you offer Sasha and Nelson jobs here, too?"

Fran nodded. "But they said no. Sasha said she'd stay with Candy and ask for a raise, and Nelson, well, who knows what Nelson wants? As soon as Sasha said no, he followed her lead. I've reached out to him again, but he's not returning my calls."

From her station nearby, Opal butted in: "Don't get me started on those two. Sasha and Nelson were always sticking their heads together and whispering. It was super annoying."

"Opal," Fran said. "Don't be insensitive."

"About what? Oh." She shrugged. "Well, it doesn't change the fact that she was annoying as hell."

Alice caught two of the other stylists glancing at each other, reacting to Opal's comment. One of them frowned. The other shook her head. Apparently, Opal had already made an impression on her new colleagues.

Fran finished Alice's hair. "There you go. Now your hair's done."

Alice eyed herself in the mirror. Fran had done more than trim her hair—she'd given it texture. Surprisingly, her hair ended up looking more like her true self.

She smiled at Fran in the mirror. "This looks terrific. Thanks."

"The cut's on me."

"No way. Your business is new. Let me pay."

"Out of the question," Fran said. "But I hope to see you back next time."

At that moment, the front door opened and Fran excused herself, putting on a big smile as she greeted the new customer. Alice, sensing their opportunity to chat with Fran and Opal was over, headed for the exit with Ona.

On the way out, Alice noticed that there was a stack of flyers on the counter by the cash register, each one advertising the Blithedale Conservation Society. She picked up one of the flyers. Among photos of the beautiful woods was one of the conservation society staff. Silas stood in front, with his colleagues arranged behind him. One of them was Fran. The flyer listed Silas as the "founder," while Fran's title was "operational assistant."

As Ona opened the door for them, Alice glanced back at Fran.

The salon owner was bustling back to a coffee machine while Opal got the customer settled by the sinks to wash her hair. Fran looked stressed. But then who wouldn't be if they were running a brand-new salon of this size *and* volunteering to run operations for a nonprofit?

"She's busy," Ona said, guessing Alice's thoughts.

"She sure is. But only four out of eight chairs are being used."

"Busy doesn't mean successful."

Ona was right. The salon—judging by its glitz and size— was ambitious. And Fran, like Candy, had her stylists on a payroll instead of renting out chairs. She thought of Candy's financial woes. Was there even enough business in Blithedale for two hair salons to survive?

CHAPTER 11

*I*t was another slow day at Wonderland Books, which gave Alice plenty of time to read *Walden* and think about the case. She read this:

> *The book exists for us perchance which will explain our miracles and reveal new ones. The at present unutterable things we may find somewhere uttered.*

And it made her think of how answers to most questions must be out there. Finding the answers wasn't a given. But that didn't mean the truth wasn't out there. It gave her hope that they might untangle the threads of this mystery and find Sasha's killer.

As she was reflecting on this, the door to the bookstore opened, and Captain Burlap stepped inside. "I talked to Nelson. He's fine. Thanks for calling me."

He gave her a big smile, dimples appearing on his cheeks.

"And I heard through the grapevine that it's official—you're helping me with the investigation."

"Is the grapevine's name Becca?"

He laughed. "Of course. She is our local oracle. So..." He came to the counter and leaned against it, crossing his arms. "What've you found out?"

She'd already told him about her encounter with Cliff over the phone, but she fleshed out the details, and then described her visit to Fran's. He didn't interrupt. She liked that about him: he was a good listener.

When she'd finished, he said, "I don't much like the idea of Cliff trying to find the killer."

"But you encourage me to snoop around."

"That's different," he said with a shrug. "I trust you won't go nuts on me and break someone's skull."

"Well, you never know."

The image of her as a big bruiser was so unlikely that it made them both smile.

She said, "But what if Cliff is right? Were Sasha and Nelson having an affair?"

"I'm looking into the possibility, but when I spoke with him earlier today, Nelson denied the idea. He's cagey about it. Though that might have more to do with me than him. I get the sense he doesn't trust us cops very much."

"Like Cliff."

Burlap nodded. "Cliff's had run-ins with the police before, so naturally, that makes him wary. But for the sake of argument, let's say Cliff is on to something. Let's imagine Sasha and Nelson were having an affair. If Sasha broke off the affair, then maybe Nelson would have a motive. But if there was an affair, it's more likely that Cliff has a motive for murder."

"A motive for murdering Nelson," Alice said. "But Sasha? He clearly loved her."

"I agree. It feels wrong, even though statistics suggest Cliff is the most likely suspect. In any case, I need to keep tabs on Nelson—for his own safety. I'll go see if I can pay him a visit in town."

He meant Tilbury Town, the much larger county seat about an hour away. Many people there considered Blithedale a bucolic backwater, devoid of the shopping, restaurants, and nightlife you'd want in a thriving town. Which was, to Alice, why Blithedale was so appealing: it had held on to its woodsy simplicity.

Burlap told her he was off to visit Candy before heading back to Tilbury Town, then levered himself off her counter.

"Thanks for the insights, Alice. It's always a pleasure talking to you."

She watched him go, glad she could work with a lawman who was so thoughtful and likable. It made her even more determined to solve the murder.

CHAPTER 12

*A*fter closing the bookstore for the day, Alice went to the diner. She'd agreed to meet Ona for dinner. Becca was busy serving customers. She and Susan seemed to skate across the floor, flitting from one table to the next, taking orders and delivering food with uncanny speed. Alice was impressed. If she had to move so fast to bring books to her customers, she'd be exhausted within minutes.

She headed for the counter and sat down, then realized who she'd sat next to.

"Candy."

Candy, putting down the coffee she'd been sipping, greeted her with a smile—a big one.

"I just got the best news ever," she said. "Captain Burlap says I can reopen tomorrow. The salon is no longer an active crime scene."

"That is great news," Alice said. "You're back in business."

"Well..." Candy's face fell. "I've got a lot of work to do to get back on track. With three of my stylists gone..."

"Three?"

"Fran, Opal, and—" Candy looked stricken. "And Sasha, of course. I could never replace her. She was a genuine talent. Her clients loved her."

"What about Fran and Opal? How're they as stylists?"

"Fran's like Sasha—an incredibly talented stylist. She was my second in command, opening the salon some mornings and even helping me with the bookkeeping. I expected her to take over the business one day. But Opal…" She shook her head. "That girl wants an easy ride. She's convinced that snapping selfies will lead to fortune and fame."

Alice could only nod in agreement—Candy's description of Opal was spot on.

"Oh, I shouldn't be so tough on Opal," Candy said. "She's young. When I was her age, I was the same."

"Only you didn't have social media back then."

Candy chuckled. "True. But you'd better believe I found other ways to distract myself."

"What about Nelson?"

Candy put a finger in her hair and twirled a strand of it, a girlish gesture that gave Alice a brief impression of what the salon owner might've looked like as a younger woman.

"Nelson," she said. "He's a bit of an enigma."

She described him as quiet, introverted, even borderline antisocial. He'd never join the others for drinks after work. He did his work, then headed home to Tilbury Town.

"But he's a talented stylist—and I can tell he gets joy from the work. In recent weeks, I noticed that he and Sasha had talked more, and sometimes they left together, as if they were going out together."

"Like they were dating?"

"Oh, not like girlfriend-boyfriend. I'm pretty sure Nelson is gay. Besides, Sasha wasn't cagey about the two of them going for drinks, and she had that big beefy boyfriend of hers, Cliff. They seemed to suit each other." Candy heaved a big sigh. "Poor guy."

Alice reflected on that. Candy made a good point. If Sasha had wanted to cheat on Cliff, she would've been more careful. Her behavior suggested she and Nelson were just good friends. Still, that wouldn't keep Cliff from blaming Nelson.

Alice explained to Candy that she was worried about Nelson. She left out why. She didn't want to suggest to Candy that Cliff was a danger—only that she'd called several times with no luck. Besides, Captain Burlap seemed on top of it. Still, she would love to talk to Nelson—really talk to him—and see if he knew something about Sasha that might hint at *who* killed her and *why*.

Candy said, "Why don't I try? After all, I'm his boss, and who doesn't answer the phone when the boss calls?"

She brought out her phone, found Nelson in her contacts, and hit the call button.

"It's ringing," she said. Then she said, "Oh, hi, Nelson, it's Candy. I've got Alice here. She wants to talk to you."

She handed the phone to Alice.

"Nelson," Alice said. "Hi."

"Hi."

Silence.

"Uh, I wanted to talk to you because of Cliff—you know, Sasha's boyfriend."

"I know."

"You know?"

"I know. Captain Burlap came to my place and told me. I know. Anything else?"

"Uh…" About a dozen questions. But his reticence gave her pause. A deep disquiet told her not to poke her nose into his business. "No. I guess not."

"OK, bye."

He hung up.

Alice handed the phone back to Candy. "He's a man of few words, isn't he?"

Candy quirked a smile. "A man of the fewest words."

CHAPTER 13

*A*fter Candy left, Alice ordered Becca's famous meatloaf special with mashed potatoes, green beans, and cranberry sauce. One for herself and one for Ona, who was due to arrive at any moment. The dinner rush was settling into a regular groove, giving Becca a moment to grab a glass of water and talk to Alice.

Alice thought about what Burlap had called Becca: the town oracle. Which was just about right. After all, any gossip flowing through Blithedale would run through the diner.

"Candy compared herself to Opal," Alice said. "Which surprised me. Opal seems to prefer scrolling on her phone to actually doing work. Candy obviously works hard."

"Incredibly hard," Becca agreed. "But it's true—she was pretty happy-go-lucky when she was young. Things got hard for her pretty early on. Her father struggled with substance abuse, her husband died in a work-related accident, and their only son, who had a tough time after his dad's death, got into trouble with the cops and even lived on the streets for a while."

"Wow, I had no idea."

"Things are better now, of course. Her son cleaned up and has a steady job in Tilbury Town. Candy threw herself into work after her husband's death, and after years of keeping her nose to the grindstone, she turned that salon into a success—or at least, she turned it into a business that pays the bills."

"It's not a lucrative business, is it?"

Becca laughed. "None of us are becoming millionaires in Blithedale. But that's all right. We're rich in other ways."

Alice smiled. It was so true. She felt richer than a millionaire. After all, she had the best friends she could imagine, her dream bookstore, and a life in the middle of a stunning forested landscape.

She turned her thoughts back to the investigation.

"Tell me about the other two—Nelson and Fran."

"Nelson's new to town," Becca said. "He came for the job at Candy's. I hear he lives in Tilbury Town. But I don't think he's lived in this part of the state for long. He strikes me as a city guy."

"You mean he's fashionable?"

Becca nodded. "Chic."

The word felt right. Nelson wore his clothes with a sense of purpose. Most guys around Blithedale wore flannels and jeans—and not always without holes—except the mayor, of course, who insisted on donning that Mark Twain suit.

Thinking of the mayor sent a vibration of annoyance through her. She couldn't forget how rude he'd been to her, and all because he was so preoccupied with making money off that development project. The mayor had always been nice to her. It was depressing how money could make people so nasty.

"And Fran," Becca continued, "she's a local. She started off at a salon in Tilbury Town and then got a job at Candy's place. She grew in her role. Over time, she acted almost like a business partner to Candy, and everyone assumed she'd take over the salon when Candy retired." Becca chuckled. "If that ever happens."

"Now that she's won the lottery, I guess things may change."

"They may," Becca said with a shrug. "Or they may not. Candy's put her whole life into that little salon. I doubt she'll make any big changes. But the money will be a big help, no doubt. A big help. Especially since she'll need to hire new stylists."

"That's right, Sasha's gone, and so are Fran and Opal."

Becca nodded. "Leaving only Nelson."

At that moment, Ona joined them at the counter and the talk turned to tiny houses—Ona had sold another one of her miniature homes. Alice welcomed the change of topic. But she couldn't stop thinking through what she'd learned.

No one seemed to say anything negative about Sasha. Nor did she pose a threat to anyone. So why would someone want to murder her? Who was hiding the truth? Of all the people involved in this case, one person stood out as being the most secretive...

Nelson.

CHAPTER 14

*G*etting Nelson on the phone might be difficult—and weaseling information out of him next to impossible—but Alice knew where to find him the next morning. Candy was reopening the salon. As her only remaining employee, Nelson would surely show up for work.

This was her chance to talk to him.

After breakfast at the diner, she and Ona wandered up Main Street. Candy's Hair Salon was open. The sign in the window said so, and through the glass, the shadowy outlines of people stood clustered together.

"Oh, good, Candy already has customers," she said.

Ona came to a standstill. "Alice..."

There was a note of alarm in Ona's voice.

"What?"

Then Alice recognized the shadowy outline of the "customer" inside: giant shoulders and a back as broad as gorilla's.

"Crap," Alice said. "Cliff. He beat us to it."

She hurried to the door, flinging open the door and stepping inside. Candy was standing in front of Cliff, blocking the way to Nelson near the back.

Candy said, "Now, look here, buddy. I understand you're upset. You're grieving. But coming after Nelson is crazy."

"I know what he did."

"You know diddly-squat. Nelson didn't kill Sasha. He's grieving, too—just like everyone else."

Cliff clenched his massive fists. "Not everyone."

"Well, all right. Not everyone." Candy sighed. "But Nelson wouldn't hurt the one person who was his friend. Tell him, Nelson." Candy, keeping her eyes on Cliff, said this over her shoulder. "Go ahead, tell him how much Sasha meant to you."

Nelson stared at Cliff. He hadn't moved.

"Nelson..." Cliff growled. "Talk."

"I don't need this."

The light from outside flashed across Nelson's glasses as he turned. In a moment, he'd bounded out the back, vanishing from sight. Cliff cursed and shoved Candy aside, sending her crashing into a shelf with hairsprays.

Cliff clomped after Nelson.

Alice set off in pursuit.

Behind her, she heard Ona say, "Candy, are you all right?"

The back door of the salon led to a room with a kitchenette, shelves with supplies, and a couch—a break room for staff. A door to a bathroom stood ajar. Another swung on its hinges, opening up to the outside world. Alice stepped down the backstairs and hit the ground behind the salon. The woods began here. She recognized the trail she and Ona had seen the nighttime burglar take to get away from them.

An engine revved, and something shot past Alice, nearly knocking her down. Cliff lumbered in its wake, giving chase. But the vehicle—an avocado-green Vespa—sped up, shooting upward along the path and into the woods, carrying Nelson farther and farther away.

"Wow," Alice said. "I didn't realize Vespas could go so fast."

"That bastard," Cliff growled.

He turned on his heels and jogged around the building, no doubt heading for Main Street to get his motorcycle. Alice hoped he wouldn't catch up with Nelson. In Cliff's mind, Nelson's escape no doubt looked suspicious.

But if Cliff came after me, she thought, *wouldn't I run, too?*

CHAPTER 15

hen Alice returned to the salon, Candy and Ona were gone. She looked around, finally seeing them. Through the window, she could see them standing outside on the sidewalk.

Then she heard the voices. Shouting.

Oh, no.

What if Nelson, for whatever reason, had driven his Vespa around to Main Street, hoping to outmaneuver his opponent, and then Cliff had caught him?

But as she pulled open the door and the full force of the yelling hit her, she saw it had nothing to do with Nelson and Cliff. In fact, Cliff stood on the sidewalk near Candy and Ona, staring at the scene in front of them.

The commotion was across the street at the construction site. A worker in a hard hat stood by a jackhammer, staring at the drama, while another sat on his bulldozer with a frown on his face. Mayor MacDonald waved at them, yelling, "Keep going, boys—keep going!"

But in front of the construction site, a crowd had gathered. Silas, standing on a box, led them in a call-and-response protest. He spoke through a megaphone. "When I say 'Blithedale,' you say 'Woods.'"

Then he hollered, "Blithedale."

"Woods," the crowd chanted back.

"Blithedale."

"Woods."

"Whose woods?" he said.

"Our woods!" the crowd roared.

Silas said, "Sheriff Cutter is on his way. He's shutting this site down. For good."

"Lies," Mayor MacDonald yelled. "There's no need to stop."

"Ask the sheriff, mayor—he's here now."

Alice scanned the crowd, then saw, down the street, a police cruiser parked by the curb. Sheriff Cutter trudged toward the crowd, his hands gripping his belt, as if it was all that kept it from falling down.

Mayor MacDonald turned to him. "Sheriff, I'm glad you're here. This man is claiming, falsely, that the work will shut down, but—"

Sheriff Cutter said, "He's right. The development company's paperwork isn't in order."

Mayor MacDonald's face went rigid with shock. "But they assured me..."

"I'm sure they did, mayor. But until the proper paperwork is done, this construction site needs to shut down. I'm pulling the plug."

The mayor rounded on Silas. "You."

Silas smirked. "Now, Mayor MacDonald, don't be a sore loser. We all—"

"All you do is say *no*. All you do is say *stop*. If it were up to you, this town would grind to a halt."

Mayor MacDonald's face went purple. His body shook. He looked like he might have a stroke, and Alice took a step toward the curb, intending to cross the street to him in case he needed help.

But he didn't collapse. Instead, he strode up to Silas, grabbed him by the shirt, and yanked him off the box.

Silas went flying, hitting the sidewalk hard. For a moment, he looked dazed, staring up at the mayor in surprise. Then the surprise congealed into anger and he shot to his feet, like a boxer.

He brought up his fists and swung at the mayor. The mayor ducked, taking the punch on the shoulder. He came up jabbing at Silas, and the punch connected with his face. Silas staggered back. He put a hand to his nose as blood trickled down.

"That's enough," Sheriff Cutter bellowed, stepping between the two men. "Cut it out, or I'll haul you both down to the lockup."

"He started it," Silas said, his voice sounded muffled and nasal.

"No, you," Mayor MacDonald spat. "You've been hounding me for days now, harassing me, making my life a living hell."

As he spoke, the mayor shook and his face turned an even deeper shade of purple. This time, Alice was sure he'd have a stroke. But Sheriff Cutter patted the mayor on the arm and said, "Mayor, you'd better walk away. Or Silas here will have grounds for pressing charges. Which I'm sure he doesn't want to do." He glanced back at Silas and frowned. "Does he?"

Several of Silas's followers had gathered around him—all, she noticed, young women—and they were handing him tissues to stanch his bleeding nose. Silas gave the sheriff a measured look. Then said, "No, I don't want to press charges."

"Good," Sheriff Cutter said. "Now, get out of my sight. Or I'll charge you both with disturbing the peace."

Mayor MacDonald, his face less flushed, strode off, muttering under his breath.

The conservation society followers—minus Fran, Alice noticed—clustered around Silas.

"That was quite a show," Ona said.

"I've never seen the mayor do a thing like that," Candy said. "I'm shocked."

Ona shrugged. "The guy's full of surprises."

"It's this development project he invested in," Alice said. "He must have a lot riding on it."

Candy nodded. "I think that's it. From what I hear, he bet the entire farm."

"Still," Ona said, "it's no way to behave."

Alice knew Ona and the mayor didn't see eye to eye, but she also agreed: just because the man was stressed about money didn't give him the right to hurt Silas. Money could never justify hurting someone.

Cliff, still standing nearby, snorted. "Fools," he said and headed for his motorbike. But by the time he got on it, he looked around, gazing up and down Main Street, clearly at a loss. His shoulders sank, a look of defeat on his face. Nelson would be long gone by now.

Alice was relieved. She didn't have to worry about Cliff catching Nelson and meting out his own form of crazy justice. But Silas was the one she was interested in now.

Exactly why he objected to a new building going up, Alice couldn't fully understand. It was obviously related to the woods. But how did building on a preexisting lot affect the Blithedale Woods?

She would have to find out.

CHAPTER 16

While Ona excused herself to go back to the inn, Alice stayed behind, waiting for the conservation society followers to disperse. When they did, she approached Silas.

"Are you all right?" she asked him.

Silas dabbed at his nose with a wadded-up tissue.

"Oh, this? It's just a bloody nose. I've had worse."

Alice almost rolled her eyes at his macho tone. But she hoped to get him to talk, and eye-rolling wouldn't make him open up.

"You won," she said. "That must feel good."

"We didn't win. This is a temporary reprieve—a pause— but you'll see, within a few days, the company will fix the paperwork and the construction crew will start again. We won a battle, but we may still lose the war."

"What war? I have to admit, I don't understand why putting up another building on Main Street is such a problem."

"They plan to cut down the woods."

"I've heard that," Alice said. "But the property only stretches as far as the woods…"

Silas eyed her, as if he were assessing her somehow. "You want to see for yourself?"

"I do."

"All right." He beckoned to her. "Then follow me."

He moved alongside the chain-link fence that ringed the construction zone, passing down a weed-choked alley that once separated the Townsend Developments offices from the other buildings on Main Street. Through the wire fence, Alice saw mounds of gravel, deep holes gouged out of the earth, and shovels left standing in the dirt. The construction site stretched back farther than she'd thought. The fence ended where the Blithedale Woods began.

"They're building right up to the edge of the forest," she remarked.

"If only," Silas said.

Again, he beckoned for her to follow.

He moved deeper into the woods. Under the thick canopy, the shadows deepened into a gloomy darkness. The massive tree trunks shielded the undergrowth from the sun. Moss-grown boulders rose from the dirt like the arched backs of sleeping giants. A silvery creek trickled past them, burbling as it went.

Alice wrapped her arms around her, hugging herself against the sudden chill. She glanced at Silas, who'd stopped. He had his back to her, so she couldn't see what he was doing?

"You really want to know the truth?" he asked.

"I do."

"The truth is here."

He turned around and raised a stick. Sharpened at one end, it looked like a stake, and Alice stumbled backward, imagining a murderous attack, a stab through the heart. But Silas held the stick up, waving it back and forth.

Orange paint smeared the flat end, making it easy to spot in the gloom.

"What is it?"

"It's a surveyor stake. There's another one over there."

He jerked a thumb over his shoulder and she saw a similar stake stuck in the ground 20 feet away. Now, looking around, she saw several more spread through the woods.

Alice said, "But what are surveyor stakes doing inside the Blithedale Woods?"

"The mayor's precious development project involves tearing down these trees." He gestured toward the rushing water. "And filling in that creek."

"But that's not possible. Building here must be against the town's zoning regulations."

Silas raised an eyebrow. "You mean the ones set by the zoning board, which the mayor chairs?" He tossed the surveyor stake aside. "He lobbied the others on the board to make an exception."

Alice felt outrage rise in her. "But that's a complete conflict of interest."

Silas shrugged. "Nothing new under the sun. For years, the mayor has been running Blithedale according to his own needs. His real estate company, which has a monopoly, has benefited again and again from decisions he's made as a mayor."

Alice remembered Ona's conflict with Mayor MacDonald: her tiny houses had grown in popularity, but the mayor felt that homes—and businesses—with a smaller footprint harmed the real estate market. His market. So he'd made it illegal to construct a tiny house within the town limits. Or rather, *he* hadn't—the town council's zoning board had. It was why tiny houses like Sasha's and the Woodlander Bar's were located deep in the woods.

The zoning board had made one exception: Alice's tiny house bookshop, Wonderland Books. But even that proved how Mayor MacDonald conducted business: he'd liked Alice, and liked the idea of a bookstore on Main Street, so he'd allowed it.

"I'm shocked," she said.

"But not surprised?"

She nodded. "But not surprised, no."

This changed her perspective, not only on the mayor's behavior but also the conservation society's protests. It made her think of Sasha and how passionate she'd been about the nonprofit's work to protect the woods.

"Sasha knew about this, didn't she?"

"Of course," Silas said. "We all do."

"She wanted to play a role in stopping this development project."

"She did. In fact, after you changed the rules for the lottery, she hoped to win so she could donate the prize money to the conservation society."

"That must've made you happy to hear."

"Naturally. We need every dollar we can get if we're going to take on big business."

"But you didn't always agree…"

Silas frowned. "Everyone's entitled to their opinion. Anyway, we can all agree that the Blithedale Woods are not only beautiful but also a significant ecosystem. There are woodpeckers and owls here, species that are vanishing from our forests. Look around. What if all this—" He spread out his hands. "—becomes a paved-over urban landscape?"

She looked around. The idea of tearing down the forest made her sick to her stomach. How could anyone justify such destruction?

Then she glanced back at Silas.

He's smooth, she thought. *He completely changed the subject.*

"About Sasha," she said, persisting. "She seemed so committed. So do you. I can't imagine why the two of you would fight."

"We didn't fight," Silas said, dismissing the idea with the wave of a hand. "She gave a lot of money to the conservation society, and that was wonderful. She also devoted a lot of her time to our work. Also wonderful. But she seemed to believe that she was entitled to play a part in decision-making."

"And why wasn't she?"

Silas bristled. "She was a donor. She was a volunteer. But she wasn't staff."

"Sorry, I'm not familiar with how the conservation society works…"

"Our staff members are all volunteers."

"Like Sasha? And like Fran?"

"Fran is a permanent staff member. Permanent staff members commit to certain hours every week. In exchange, they are part of the strategy and planning committee. Which I chair. Sasha, as a non-staff volunteer, could come and go as she pleased, but she didn't sit on the committee."

"Even if she donated a lot of money?"

"Money isn't everything," he snapped. "How would you feel if someone who donated to the Blithedale Future Fund suddenly stepped in and demanded to make decisions?"

Obviously irritated, Silas turned away. He walked over to the nearest surveyor's stake and yanked it out of the ground.

As she watched him remove the stakes one-by-one, she thought of what he'd said. He was right, of course. Mayor MacDonald had played the money card, demanding to influence the lottery because he'd donated to the Blithedale Future Fund, and Alice had resented it.

But even though Silas made a good point, she wondered

about the parallels between him and Mayor MacDonald. The mayor chaired the zoning board and ran the town council like a fiefdom. Silas, president of the conservation society, also controlled a little kingdom. Both demanded fealty from their followers.

The two men clashed because they had conflicting interests. But maybe they also clashed because they were, in many respects, mirror images of each other.

Alice refused to take either man's side. But looking at the issues at stake, she had no doubt about what needed to be done. The Blithedale Woods must be protected. Sasha had understood that. The question was, had it gotten her killed?

CHAPTER 17

The next day, Alice expanded her display of nature books to cover two tables. She'd also emailed the conservation society with an offer to keep a pile of their promotional materials in the bookstore. Fran herself stopped by in the afternoon, handing Alice a stack of flyers.

"Thanks for dropping these off in person," Alice said.

"I've been meaning to come by, anyway. I need a book on business management."

Alice showed Fran the small section of business books. As Fran read the back blurbs on books, a frown clouded her face. Fatigue ringed her eyes. She shifted from one foot to another, as if an itch bothered her, and she sighed as she replaced one of the books and picked another.

"Is this any good?"

She held up a book called *Traction: Get a Grip on Your Business.*

"I haven't read it," Alice admitted.

Fran read the back, then flicked through the pages.

"I guess this'll do." She headed toward the counter to pay, but stopped at the nature display table. Running her hands over several books with slow reverence, she reached *Walden*, and stopped. She picked up a copy of the book and, for a moment, a smile lifted the veil of fatigue. "Gosh, it's been so long since I read this…"

"I'm reading it now. If you reread it, I'd love to talk about it over coffee sometime. What's better than a good book, coffee, and conversation?"

Fran stared at the copy of *Walden*. Then pressed it firmly to her chest. "You know what? It's a date. I have a feeling I'll love revisiting Walden Pond."

As Alice rang up the books, they chatted about the successful protest and the conservation society's ability to stop the development project. Alice shared how shocked she'd been that the construction zone extended into the woods.

Fran nodded. "More people need to know. Silas is talking to Todd Townsend today to get the story in *The Blithedale Record*. He's also talking to national media to see if we can get them to cover the news. The more people know about this, the better chance we have of saving the woods."

"It must be gratifying to make progress," Alice said, "but also so much work."

"It is," Fran admitted. "I'm Silas's administrator, supporting his activism and ecology work, and also keeping tabs on the volunteers."

"Like Sasha?"

"Yeah, Sasha was a volunteer."

Alice studied Fran. Had that been a grimace she suppressed?

"Anything wrong?"

Fran shook her head. "No, it's just…"

"Something about Sasha?"

"Look, I'm sorry about what happened to her. It's awful. But even thinking about her role in the conservation society makes me exhausted. She was constantly jumping into conversations, meddling in projects, and making suggestions."

"She did seem eager to help."

"Eager? It was annoying. For those of us spending many hours a day on the work itself, it was very frustrating to have Sasha ride in on her high horse and tell us what to do. She could be so—" Fran clammed up. Then quickly handed over money to pay for the books, mumbling, "I don't mean to speak ill of the dead."

"Don't worry, Fran. It's OK to express your frustration about someone's behavior, even if they died. And I can see how Sasha's involvement must've been aggravating—for you and for Silas."

She snorted. "Silas. He never bore the brunt of Sasha's meddling. Besides, he can be forgiving."

"Forgiving?" Alice said, handing Fran her change.

"Mostly, Silas is unyielding. But sometimes, Silas can be remarkably accommodating."

"Sometimes?" Instinct made her add, "When there's an attractive woman involved?"

Fran didn't respond to that, but her silence was a loud and clear *yes*.

"Were Silas and Sasha…?"

Fran gave her a sharp look. "Sleeping together? Did Silas tell you that?" She studied Alice with a fierce intensity. Then looked away and said, "She wasn't his type. Besides, she had Cliff. And I think—"

Again, she cut herself off. She grabbed her books, fumbling with them and dropping *Walden* onto the floor. Flustered, she bent down and retrieved it and hurried to the door.

"Uh, thanks," she mumbled on her way out.

Wow, Alice thought. *That touched a nerve.*

CHAPTER 18

*A*fter closing Wonderland Books for the day, Alice was still thinking about Fran and Silas. So it felt as if the universe were in tune with her thoughts as she stepped into the Pemberley Inn looking for Ona and caught sight of Silas in the backyard.

The stars might be aligned, she thought. *But let's also face it: Blithedale's a small place. Bumping into someone hardly qualifies as fate.*

The backyard of the Pemberley Inn contained an entire village of tiny houses. Ona could build them quicker than she could sell them. Partly because of the mayor's efforts to block her sales, but more than anything because of her talent and hard work.

Alice went through the lounge and out the doors to the porch on the other side. At the bottom of the steps, she found Ona shaking hands with Silas.

Silas said hello and goodbye to Alice. "I have to head back to work. We have a real shot at shutting down this building project—but every second counts."

She wished him luck, and he waved as he walked away, following the back porch to the gate that led out to Main Street. Once he was out of sight, Ona grabbed Alice's hands and squeezed them.

"He's going to help me with my tiny houses," she said.

"Help you? But how? The town council—"

"—have changed their minds."

"Mayor MacDonald, changing his mind? That sounds like a big transformation."

"Oh, not him. But he's not a dictator, you know. We do have other people on the council, and they've been appalled to learn how he's manipulated them for his own gain. They've revisited the regulations around square footage of businesses. In fact, one of them cited Wonderland Books as an example of how—and I quote—'it's not about quantity but quality.' Nice, huh?" She grinned at Alice. "They're voting on changes to the code in the next few days. The conservation society—and Silas, in particular—played a big part in pushing the town council to change."

Alice couldn't help but smile at Ona's enthusiasm. Thinking back to her own bookstore and its expanded display of nature books—which, she had to admit, was inspired by the conservation efforts—it occurred to her that Silas was having a big impact on Blithedale. When she mentioned it to Ona, her friend laughed.

"He is having an impact," she agreed. "And not just on businesses. Have you noticed how many of the conservation society's new members are women? That's not just because they care about the woods. He's got a certain charm."

"Funny you should mention that…"

She told Ona about her conversation with Fran, and how flustered Fran had become.

"It made me wonder whether she has feelings for Silas."

"Feelings?" Ona snorted. "Honestly, that woman's had a crush on Silas for years. But she's never worked up the courage to tell him."

"You think he knows?"

Ona shrugged. "Silas is one of those men who assumes most women have a crush on him. He might know. But does he care?"

"Ouch. I thought you liked him."

"I like what he does to protect our woods. And to advocate for my tiny houses. But do I like all of him, the whole human being?" She shook her head. "I wouldn't want to spend a lot of time with him. I'd feel suffocated by his big ego."

Alice considered this for a moment—and what Ona had said about Fran. Seen through the lens of the murder investigation, Silas's ego and treatment of women might be an important clue to the killer's motive.

"What if Fran made her feelings clear, but someone else got in the way?"

"Sasha? I don't know. She seemed pretty committed to Cliff."

"Sure. But hear me out. Silas, convinced every woman must love him, pursues Sasha. Maybe Sasha wasn't genuinely interested, but she saw an opportunity to gain more influence in the conservation society. Fran would've noticed how Silas paid attention to Sasha, of course, and she would've felt threatened."

She considered how Fran had followed Silas at the Woodlander Bar. There had been a kind of power dynamic in their body language toward each other, as he turned his back on her. What if Silas had rejected her, yet she continued to follow him, hoping to change his mind—or his heart?

"I'd give a lot to see them together."

"Silas and Fran?" Ona said. "That's easy. They're staging a rally tomorrow—a campaign ahead of the vote on the town's development code."

"Perfect. What do you say we check it out?"

"You got it."

CHAPTER 19

Silas and the conservation society volunteers had gathered outside of the diner the next morning, a sea of placards held high. One said, "A big change for tiny houses." Another, "Sustainable living in Blithedale NOW." But Alice's favorite was the one Fran held, which said, "Big dreams come in small sizes."

She nudged Ona. "You should steal that as a tagline for your tiny house business."

"I like it, but—" She gestured toward the diner. "—I don't think *he* does."

A few paces away from where they stood, the door to the diner opened and Mayor MacDonald stepped out, his face clenched with anger.

"Enough," he growled at Silas. "Are you deliberately persecuting me?"

Silas laughed. "Why would I waste time on you? I've got bigger fish to fry."

Alice winced. Already the two men were raring to fight.

The mayor stepped up to Silas, gesturing angrily at a

nearby placard. "Tiny houses aren't the answer. No one will come do business or live here, if everyone has to live in a dollhouse." It was almost as if he sensed Ona nearby, because he spun around and jabbed an accusing finger at her. "You put him up to this, didn't you? You're trying to drum up support for your business."

Ona fended off the accusation with the wave of a hand, refusing to rise to the bait. Nearby, Todd Townsend of *The Blithedale Record* snapped a photo with his camera.

Denied a confrontation, Mayor MacDonald turned back to Silas. But instead of Silas, he faced Fran. Fran's face was set in a cold, hard glare.

"Step away, mayor," she said. "Or we'll call the sheriff."

"You'll what?"

"And this time, we won't hesitate to press charges."

Mayor MacDonald's mustache wobbled as he muttered something unintelligible. Finally, he strode off, but not without a parting volley: "This'll be the death of Blithedale. The death!"

The crowd watched him leave. He was still within earshot when the conservation society volunteers cheered. Alice thought, even at a distance, she could see the mayor's shoulders tense. And then fall.

Did he realize how far he'd fallen in people's esteem? He'd been taking advantage of his position for years, but now, with the curtain finally lifted, people seemed to see all his flaws more clearly, and they'd had enough.

It was only right that the mayor's abuse of power should be exposed, but Alice couldn't help but feel sad. Sad for the mayor. And sad for Blithedale that it had come to this: placards raised, public humiliation, fist fights. Who wanted things to end this way?

"Great, isn't it?" Todd said.

He'd been standing nearby, and in between whipping out his phone and snapping photos, he'd been scribbling furiously on a notepad.

"Nothing like a bit of drama."

"Well, I'm glad someone's happy," Alice said.

"Oh, come off it. You know, as well as I do, that everyone in town will devour my next story as quickly as they wolf down Becca's meatloaf."

"Does that make it good?"

He shrugged. "Good. Bad. What does it all mean, anyway? It's all semantics, better left to academics. I'm just trying to run a news site and sell ad space."

He excused himself to go talk to Silas, leaving Alice to wonder about whether Blithedale's newshound would ever develop a stronger sense of morals. Probably not. As she watched him talk to Silas, she noticed Silas barking something at Fran.

"But I want to help with the protest..." she said.

"Don't be selfish," he said. "This is about the cause, not your own wants and needs."

Fran nodded, looking defeated. "Sure, Silas. I'll go right away. See you back at the office."

She turned around and hurried off, while Silas, hardly taking notice, continued to talk to Todd. Down the street, Fran turned to gaze back at Silas, a look of desperation on her face. Not that Silas noticed.

Alice stared at him. She was seeing him in a new light. He might do important conservation work, but his behavior toward Fran was appalling.

Ona nudged her.

"Hey, you're oozing anger. What's up?"

"Silas."

Ona laughed. "Getting a different impression of our local saint?"

Alice nodded. She was getting a very different impression indeed. But he wasn't the only one making an impression. She was seeing something new in Fran, too: desperation. And desperation could make people do drastic things.

CHAPTER 20

*A*t the crack of dawn the next day, birdsong woke Alice. Birdsong—and something else, too. A loud thwack, thwack, thwack that she was familiar with, though not usually at this early hour.

She slipped out of bed, and after taking a quick shower and running a brush through her hair, she pulled on a hoodie, jeans, jacket, and sneakers. Before heading out the door, she grabbed her copy of *Walden* from her bedside table. She shoved it into the inner pocket of her jacket.

Never leave home without a book.

As she went down the old staircase outside her room, she greeted the framed prints on the walls, each one an artist's rendition of a Jane Austen character. To the casual observer, these might look like vintage portraits. But Alice knew better. Ona, a die-hard Janeite, had commissioned them for her inn.

Mr. Bingley and Mr. Knightley gazed back at her. She said hello to Emma Woodhouse and Marianne Dashwood. And made a face at George Wickham.

The reception area was empty, as she'd guessed it would

be, so she dashed through the house to the inn's back lounge. This was where Ona kept her Jane Austen board games and reading material for guests—countless editions of Austen's works, from *Sense and Sensibility* to *Lady Susan*.

She peered out of the lounge's windows to the back porch beyond, then pulled open the door and stepped out into fresh air, still heavy with morning dew.

Droplets of water glistened on the roofs of the tiny houses. A cardinal landed on the gable of a miniature Nantucket-style cottage. As Alice moved down into the miniature village, the bird took flight, flitting off to the nearby woods.

Ona stood over a piece of wood laid across a weather-worn trestle table, hammering nails into one side to fasten it to another plank. She looked up as Alice approached and grinned.

"Morning," she said.

"The woodpecker is awake early."

"Oh." Ona glanced up at the inn. "I hope I didn't bother the guests. I just have so much work to get through today."

Alice looked around. "It doesn't look like you're running out of stock."

Ona's grin widened. "Look again."

Alice looked again, and now she saw that several tiny houses bore signs that said, "Sold." She spun around. "What? When did this happen?"

"Yesterday. Cool, right? And I've got several tailor-made orders to fill. All of this is thanks to Silas. The conservation society's campaign to encourage more sustainable housing in Blithedale has inspired people to buy tiny houses. Business is booming."

"After all this time…" Alice couldn't help but grin, too, as excitement buzzed in her gut. She knew how much this meant to Ona. "I can't believe things are finally changing. But then it is about time."

Ona nodded. "I kinda lost hope. But now I think there's a real chance that the town council could change its tune. In fact, they're deciding within the next day or so. Mayor MacDonald has a full mutiny on his hands."

"Do you think Blithedale may get a new mayor?"

"Whoa, Alice, now you're talking treason." Ona laughed. "But seriously, a few months ago, I wouldn't have believed it could be possible. Now, I do. Assuming a good candidate came forward to challenge Mayor MacDonald." She sighed. "Which, if I'm honest, we've never had."

Alice gave it some thought. Who could challenge Mayor MacDonald for the position as mayor? It would have to be someone who knew the community well, who people respected, and who had a knack for leadership.

She wouldn't be surprised if Silas stepped forward. But Alice hoped someone else would run. It would be nice if Blithedale could get a mayor that wasn't all male ego.

She watched Ona hammering, then turning the planks to eye her work, and Alice wondered if her friend would make a decent mayor. She knew she could do it—certainly better than Mayor MacDonald. Among the three friends, Ona was the organizer. She was the one who managed the systems underlying the Blithedale Future Fund. She'd bought this old Victorian mansion, refurbished it, and turned it into a successful inn, while also running a side hustle as a tiny house builder. Not to mention helping Alice with the occasional mystery.

But she wasn't born in Blithedale. For some people in this little town, it mattered whether you'd grown up in town. Would people choose to vote for Mayor MacDonald again because he was a local rather than choose a new, more trustworthy candidate? Would they opt for Silas because he exuded authority?

Ona looked up from her work. "Where did you go?"

Alice thought she'd better keep her thoughts to herself for now. She had a feeling Ona wasn't ready for the idea of getting into local politics.

"Oh, nothing. Just daydreaming."

"At this hour, it's early enough to call it 'dreaming.' How about some coffee?"

"And breakfast. I'm hungry. Let's go to the diner."

"You got it. But then I have to rush back and keep working. I've got lots of things to do." Ona rattled off her list of tasks, from assembling a thatched-roof tiny house to planning one inspired by a gingerbread house, plus preparing rooms at the inn for new guests. "Oh, and I almost forgot. I need to run by Fran's salon. She offered I could leave a stack of my tiny house brochures on her counter."

"Let me do it," Alice said. "I'll take the brochures to Fran."

Alice jumped at the opportunity to help her friend. Ona had plenty to see to. But it was also an excuse to talk to Fran again and maybe get another insight into her relationship with Silas—and with Sasha.

CHAPTER 21

*A*fter breakfast, Alice headed over to Fran's salon. As she stepped inside, she noticed that there were no customers. Fran and Opal stood by one of the chairs, talking. They hadn't noticed Alice yet, and she caught the tail-end of an argument.

"You want the fame without the hard work," Fran was saying. "Do you have any idea how tough it is to run a business like this? It's no good when one of the stylists slacks off."

"Whatever." Opal grabbed a purse from the shelf by the mirror and slung it over her shoulder. "You're not my mother."

And with that, she pushed past Fran, and without giving Alice more than a glance, stormed out of the salon.

Fran gazed after her. Then collapsed onto a chair and buried her head in her hands.

Alice left the tiny house brochures on the counter and headed over to Fran. "Fran, are you all right?"

Fran drew in a breath and let out a long sigh. She dropped her hands.

"Yeah, I'm fine."

Alice crouched down to put herself at Fran's height, letting the silence be an invitation to talk.

Fran sighed. "It's just work stuff."

"Hey." Alice put a hand on her shoulder. "I own a business, too. Sometimes it feels like climbing a mountain."

"More like climbing a mountain with a pile of bricks on your back."

Alice nodded, encouraging Fran to go on.

Fran said, "Truth is, I'm overwhelmed. I thought running my own salon would be fun. When I was working at Candy's, she gave me all this responsibility. I handled bookkeeping. I reorganized the business in a dozen small ways. Candy's skilled at so many things, but she's not a numbers whiz. It felt good to make improvements that made a difference. I thought this was how it would be to own my own place—every day, I'd get the gratification of fixing those little things."

"But there's no time, right?"

"Right. It's an endless series of big things, and I have no time for the small, satisfying tweaks. It's my own fault. I should've looked at Candy and learned from her own situation: she didn't have time to do all the things I was doing; that was why she needed me. I need another me."

She glanced over at the door to the salon.

Alice sensed what Fran was thinking.

"You'd hoped to bring an experienced stylist with you from Candy's—someone who could provide that extra support."

Fran nodded. "But Opal isn't me. She shows up late and when she's here, she's more interested in snapping selfies than doing the work I pay her to do. Forget about her helping me out with the business. And she's not even a star stylist, like Sasha was."

"Customers liked Sasha."

89

"They loved her. Sure, some people took convincing at first. This is a small, provincial town. Many people have old-fashioned ideas. They looked at Sasha and thought, 'She's all punk—she can't do my hair the way I like it.' But Sasha's own style had nothing to do with her ability to style hair. She could literally do anything for anyone, and once customers discovered that, they stuck with her."

"That's why you asked her to join you."

"She would've attracted a lot of customers." Fran gestured around her at the empty salon. "But look. Since Candy reopened, I can hardly attract anyone. I've got my other stylists coming to work in an hour, and we have almost no bookings. I should never have copied Candy's business model—keeping staff on payroll is almost impossible."

"You mean as opposed to renting out chairs?"

Fran nodded. "I'm not Candy. I may have to change how I do this. Before I run out of money."

Alice thought of Candy's own financial woes and wondered whether Candy herself was wise to stick with a payroll model. If Wonderland Books had to support several employees, Alice would feel an immense pressure to bring in revenue all the time. As it was, her overhead was reasonably low, because she relied so much on donated, used books, and she was the only person who needed to make a living off the business.

She said, "Why don't you switch to renting out chairs?"

"I wouldn't have been able to attract the talent I wanted."

"Someone like Sasha wouldn't have done it?"

"I don't think so. She enjoyed being hands off, not having to deal with the business side. She told me she wanted her job to be stable—and hopefully get a raise from Candy—so she could focus on her work with the conservation society."

Fran turned away, hiding some emotion.

Alice took a chance. She said, "You didn't love that she got so involved in the conservation society. You told me that. But there was another reason, too. You didn't love how close she was getting to Silas. Because you want to be close to him— you and no one else."

Fran drew in a sharp breath. Then she let it out, her shoulders slumping.

"Is it that obvious?" she muttered. She turned back to Alice, a bitter frown on her face. "I guess it is."

"But you and Silas spend so much time together, I can only imagine—"

"That he likes me?" She laughed. There was no joy in her laugh. "Yeah, we had something for a while, but then the conservation society really took off. Suddenly, we got lots of what Silas calls 'fresh blood.' Young, enthusiastic volunteers from Blithedale, Tilbury Town, and elsewhere. And why date a 40-year-old woman when you've got 23-year-olds trailing after you?"

Alice thought of Silas's followers—the young women she'd seen flocking around him—and she didn't doubt he enjoyed the attention.

"Was Sasha one of those young women?"

Fran rubbed her face with her hands. "They spent a lot of time together." She let out a long breath and then pushed herself off the chair. "Enough," she said, apparently to herself. "My business won't get better if I sit around moping. But I could use some caffeine. I'm going out back to make one of my special coffee drinks. Want one? It's delicious."

Alice hesitated. She didn't need or even want coffee, but Fran's reaction to Sasha had been ambivalent, at best. Despite Sasha being gone, Fran still seemed angry. How much anger had she felt when Sasha was alive? And had she done anything about it? Alice would like to find out. But she needed time to look around.

So she nodded. "I'd love a coffee."

"Great." Fran headed toward a door in the back. "I'll only be a few minutes."

"Take your time."

As soon as Fran was out of sight, Alice looked around the salon. Where to begin, though? Each stylist station was neat and tidy. All but one, anyway, and she guessed that one belonged to Opal. So she headed for the tall counter near the front. A tablet sat on the counter alongside brochures for the conservation society and, now, Ona's tiny houses. Alice tried the drawer below the tablet, but it was locked.

She was about to turn away when something shiny caught her eye. It was sticking out from beneath the tablet. Alice lifted the tablet and there, hidden underneath, was a small key. She fit it into the lock and turned it.

The drawer, like everything else Fran had a hand in, was well-organized. A stack of sticky notes filled the left side. A tray with pens ran across the bottom. And there was a small bowl with coins and a key ring with several keys attached, plus a pink charm. All very ordinary stuff.

Alice was about to close the drawer when she stopped and looked again.

That charm...

She pulled the key ring out. Aside from three keys, it had that pink charm attached to it, one she'd seen before. A pink lollipop. Wasn't that what she'd seen Sasha use to open Candy's salon? She wasn't 100 percent sure...

Alice dug out her phone, held up the key ring, and snapped a photo, getting close-ups of the keys and the charm. Then she put the key ring back in the drawer and shut it. She slipped the little key under the tablet again.

She took another look at her phone to make sure the photos were all right—she'd need them later to confirm whether one of the keys belonged to Candy's Hair Salon.

Looking at the photos again, though, she noticed another detail. Two of the keys were ordinary and clearly opened doors to businesses or homes. But the third belonged to a vehicle. But not just any vehicle. The handle had a half-moon shape and said, "Vespa."

A scooter. Which can sound a lot like a motorbike...

Was that what she'd heard the night the burglar got away?

"Here it is," Fran said behind her, and Alice jumped.

Alice shoved her phone into her pocket and, trying to show a big, unconcerned smile, reached for the coffee drink Fran offered her.

"Gee, thanks. You didn't need to go to all this trouble."

The drink, in fact, looked like a lot of trouble—with a mound of whipped cream on top and a swirl of chocolate syrup.

A sinking, sickening feeling in Alice's gut told her what it was before Fran revealed it.

"It's a mochaccino. Everyone loves it. In fact, Opal likes to say she came up with the 'stylist's mochaccino' idea, but I was actually the one who showed her how to make it. Now she makes them all the time."

"It looks—" Alice swallowed. "—delicious."

"It's from a mix, but you'd never know." Fran sipped her drink. "Go ahead, try it."

Alice tensed. Her stomach curled up into a tight ball. Fran was watching her. Alice stared at the mound of whipped cream and thought, *Is this how I die, sipping an excessively sweetened coffee drink?*

She couldn't think of an excuse not to taste. She licked the whipped cream, which turned out to be as sweet as cotton candy. Then she took a sip. The coffee, mixed with hot chocolate, tasted so sticky sweet that it might as well have been pure molasses.

"What do you think?"

Alice nodded, forcing her throat to keep the drink down.

Fran smiled. "See, I knew you'd love it."

CHAPTER 22

*L*eaving Fran's salon, Alice's heart hammered in her chest, and it wasn't simply because she'd consumed half her weight in processed sugar and caffeine: she'd found evidence that might point to Sasha's killer.

Her head was spinning as she headed down Main Street.

But why Fran—why would she want to kill Sasha?

Because of Silas, of course. Fran had been cagey about Silas and Sasha's relationship. If they were having an affair, then Fran would have a powerful motive to get rid of her rival. She introduced the mochaccino to Candy's. She knew how much Sasha loved it. And if one of those keys on the lollipop-charm ring opened the door to Candy's Hair Salon, then it proved that Fran could get access. As Candy's most trusted former employee, she'd know the code to the alarm system. Finally, Fran owned a Vespa, and it could so easily have been a high-powered scooter Alice heard instead of a motorcycle.

Fran was the burglar the night before Sasha died; Fran was the killer.

Motive? Check.

Means? Check.

Opportunity? Check.

Alice had to talk to Becca and Ona. Together, they had to find out if Alice's theory was correct. And if it was…

She shuddered.

If it was, then she'd found the killer.

She glanced over her shoulder at the salon and, distracted, walked right into something hard. She stumbled backward, rubbing her head where she'd collided with the lamppost or tree or whatever it was.

But it wasn't a tree, or any other object. It was a giant man.

"You all right?" Cliff said.

She nodded, staring at the giant. He stood next to his motorbike, his helmet in his hand. Either he'd just arrived or he was about to leave. Alice look around and realized where they were standing: right in front of Candy's Hair Salon.

"Uh, Cliff," she said, worried about what had brought him here, "what brings you to Candy's?"

He slipped his helmet on his head. "I came to talk to Nelson. But now I'm headed up to Sasha's place to pack up more of her things."

Alice glanced at the windows to Candy's, imagining a blood bath inside. Cliff must've seen the concern on her face, because he said, "No need to freak out. Nelson and I are good."

"You're good?"

Cliff nodded. "We're good."

He swung onto his bike. Alice looked down Main Street toward the diner and, beyond that, the Pemberley Inn. She ought to go find Becca and Ona. But if Cliff was going to Sasha's house in the woods, she would have a chance to compare the keys.

"Do you mind if I tag along?" she asked Cliff.

Even through the visor, Cliff's look of suspicion was unmistakable. "Why?"

"I've got an idea about Sasha's death. But I need to take a look at her things."

His hesitation lasted only a moment. He reached into the trunk and brought out an extra helmet. He handed it to Alice. "All right, Miss Detective," he said. "I have an idea, too. You tell me yours and I'll tell you mine."

A moment later, Alice was sitting behind Cliff, her arms around his midriff. He gunned the engine, and they roared onto Main Street, flying away from the town center—and deeper and deeper into the woods.

CHAPTER 23

The road twisted and turned as they drove deeper and deeper into the woods, trees flashing past them.

Then Cliff turned off the blacktop and onto a deeply rutted dirt road. After a mile, he turned onto the narrow, bumpy path Alice and Ona had walked down that first time. Through the trees, as the bike jolted her, she caught glimpses of houses. The homes sat far apart, but they roughly followed a line: number 14, and 15, and then 16…

Finally, they pulled up in front of Sasha's tiny house, and Cliff killed the engine. Alice swung off, dazed and rattled. Cliff, rugged as he was, swept off the bike with as much ease as Alice rolled out of her canopy bed in the morning.

"Come on inside," he said. "Let's see if we can find that clue you're looking for."

Inside the quaint tiny house, dozens of cardboard boxes stood here and there on the floor. Piles of books and cookware covered the kitchen table. Bedding lay stacked on the couch.

"Sorry about the mess," Cliff said, rubbing his neck. "It's taking me longer than expected to clear her things out."

"It takes time."

Cliff looked stricken. "Yeah, that's what they say."

Alice touched Cliff's shoulder. "Take it one step at a time."

He nodded. "She didn't actually own a lot of stuff. And she'd sold some things lately. Money was tight."

"Oh?"

"Yeah, she spent almost every penny she had on that conservation society." He sighed. "We were supposed to move in together. We'd even talked about marriage, but Sasha kept putting it off, saying she wanted to be financially stable before taking such a big step. Of course, she kept spending her money…"

There was a hint of irritation in his voice. Then he glanced at Alice and said, "I can't believe I feel annoyed. If I could have her back, I'd let her spend all our money on whatever she wanted. Whatever she wanted…"

His voice trailed off, diminishing, and he stared down at the floor.

Alice moved through the kitchen, wondering where she might find Sasha's key, so she could compare it with the one she'd found at Fran's salon. On the kitchen counter stood several jars of beverage mixes: chai, pumpkin spice latte, gingerbread latte, peppermint hot chocolate, and half a dozen others Alice hadn't even imagined were possible.

Cliff noticed her examining them. "Sasha had a terrible sweet tooth. Which Opal took advantage of."

"You mean for her social media stuff?"

But as she glanced over, she saw that a menacing frown marked his face.

"Wait a minute," she said. "What do you think Opal did?"

"Opal made the drink that killed Sasha. She knew Sasha would drink it. And Opal never liked Sasha…"

"I thought you suspected Nelson."

"Nelson and I had a talk. He's not the killer."

"How come?"

"He just isn't. Ask Nelson. He can tell you. Anyway, what was the thing you were looking for?"

Alice scanned the tiny house. It was such a mess of objects, she'd never find the keys. But Cliff had been going through everything. Maybe he'd seen it.

She described the key ring with the lollipop charm.

Cliff said, "You mean this one?"

He dug into his pocket and took out an object. It was the key ring Alice had seen Sasha use the morning she died. Alice brought out her phone and opened the photos she'd snapped at Fran's salon. She held up her phone, comparing the two key rings. Both the lollipop charms and the keys themselves looked identical.

"Where did you find that?" Cliff asked.

"At Fran's."

"She owns a Vespa?" he asked. Then had another thought. "By the way, did you see Opal there?"

"You really think she wanted to kill Sasha?" Alice said.

Cliff nodded. "They were rival hairdressers. Sasha was more talented and more popular. Opal's obsessed with popularity. Maybe she wanted less competition."

"But Opal left for Fran's salon."

"Exactly," Cliff said. "Fran wanted Sasha instead, and Opal knew she could lose her spot, and so Frank spiked the coffee drink mix."

"Actually, the mochaccino was Fran's invention."

"Fran?" Cliff's eyes widened. He repeated her name, clearly mulling it over. "Fran again…"

Aw, come on, not again.

"Oh, no you don't—I wasn't suggesting…"

Cliff's face hardened. "Yes, of course. Not Opal. Fran. The mochaccino mix. That's why you're interested in the key to Candy's. Fran still has hers. Which means she could get into the hair salon and poison the mix. In fact, Fran would've known the code to the alarm system. Sasha once told me Fran was the only person Candy trusted with her accounting and alarm system. And I bet she was happy to see Sasha disappear, so she could have that conservationist guy, Silas, all to herself." He clenched his fists. "Yeah, it all fits."

This was ridiculous. He was like a pinball bouncing from suspect to suspect. She grabbed his arm. "Cliff, be reasonable. We don't know that's what happened. In fact, we don't know enough to conclude anything."

He tore himself free. "I know. I know more than enough."

He turned and strode out of the tiny house, ducking under the lintel.

She cursed and ran after him, but as she came through the door, his motorbike roared to life. The tires dug up dirt and the bike shot forward, skidding down the path, and then Cliff revved the engine and it took off even faster. The giant man on his bike flitted between the trees. Within seconds, he was out of sight.

Alice kicked a pine cone. "What's with the men in this town!?"

She slammed the door behind her. With no motorbike or car of her own, she'd have to hoof it back to town. And she'd better hurry—because who knew what Cliff might do?

As she jogged down the path, she brought out her cell phone and speed dialed Captain Burlap. She got voicemail.

Beep.

She took a deep breath.

"Captain, I've really messed this one up..."

She then launched into a summary of what had happened,

and how she'd accidentally let loose the vengeful Cliff. And how sorry she was.

But even as she was telling her story, she was thinking, *Why am I apologizing? It's Cliff who's the crazy dude. It's Cliff who's got to pull himself together.*

CHAPTER 24

*A*t Fran's salon, Alice knocked. She tried the door handle, but it was locked. Then, cupping her hands around her eyes to peer through the window, she saw only emptiness.

The sign in the window still said, "Come In, We're Open," an ominous contradiction.

She moved around the building, looking for another way to get inside. Behind the salon, there was a back door by a row of trash cans. This door was also locked. Alice looked down and saw that she was standing on a welcome mat. She remembered the tiny key Fran had hidden under the tablet.

Maybe...just maybe...

She stooped and lifted the mat, peering underneath. A beetle escaped the sudden light, but left behind no unguarded treasure, no key.

She sighed and straightened up and then saw it. Parked near the wall on the other side of the trash cans: a Vespa. Fran's scooter. And she'd left it here.

A cold certainty came over her, one she desperately wanted to deny.

Cliff couldn't have—no, he wouldn't have...

But she refused to fool herself. She'd pointed him toward Fran, and then, like a shark smelling blood, he'd set off to pursue his prey. Where could they have gone? Who could've seen them?

She hurried around the building again to the front, and as she rounded the corner, she ran straight into Ona, colliding with her friend.

"Whoa there," Ona said, grabbing her by the shoulders. "Where are you off to?"

"I've really made a mess of things."

As quickly as she could, she told Ona about her discovery at Fran's salon and then how she'd let Cliff in on the clues, convincing him that Fran was the killer.

"And now she's gone." Alice groaned. "It's all my fault."

Ona, with her jaw set, said, "We'll find her. We'll fix this. Got it?"

Alice nodded, feeling none of the confidence Ona exuded.

Ona said, "First, we check Candy's—maybe Fran went there, or else Cliff did."

Ona grabbed her hand and led her to her pickup truck, which stood parked by the curb. Ona got into the driver's seat and Alice pulled herself into the cab on the passenger's side.

Ona revved the engine. "Let's go."

CHAPTER 25

*A*lice pulled open the door to the hair salon. Inside, it was busy. Nelson was working at one station, Candy at another, and there was a third stylist, apparently a new hire. Two other customers sat in chairs and read magazines, waiting for their turn.

But when Alice asked Candy and Nelson whether they'd seen Fran or Cliff, they both shook their heads. Alice bit her lip. What now? Where else could they have gone?

Ona came up behind her. "Let's think through Cliff's logic. Maybe it'll lead us to where he might go."

Alice shrugged. She didn't think he was acting entirely rationally, although he'd used logic to justify why he believed Fran was the killer. She thought back to her conversation with him at Sasha's place. She said, "Well, he pieced together the clues I shared, but actually, at first, he was convinced Opal was somehow implicated."

"Opal?" Ona said.

Nearby, Candy echoed her. "Opal? Of all people."

"That's what he said."

"Well," Candy said with a snort, "I wouldn't put much

faith in that idea. I mean, Cliff also believed Nelson here was guilty."

Alice looked over at Nelson, who kept his eyes on his customer and the job at hand. It was interesting that Cliff had been so convinced that Nelson killed Sasha, even chasing him through town, only to change his mind. He didn't want to say why, only that Nelson didn't do it, and that if Alice wanted to know why, she should talk to Nelson.

Alice stepped over to Nelson, who continued to ignore her.

"Nelson," she said. "Any idea where Cliff is?"

Nelson shook his head. "Nope."

"He suspected you."

Nelson frowned and glanced down at the customer, who was doing a poor job of pretending not to listen. He looked at Alice and said, "Do you mind?"

"This is important."

"So is my career."

"Fran may be in trouble. Like, life and death trouble."

Nelson eyed her suspiciously, then apologized to the client for taking a break. He jerked his head at the back door, gesturing toward the break room.

Alice and Ona followed him.

He shut the door behind them. Then crossed his arms.

"If Fran is in genuine trouble, I'll help," he said. "Now, what is it you want to know?"

"Cliff was so convinced you killed Sasha, he—"

Nelson barked a single laugh. "Right. Simply because I didn't spill all my secrets onto his lap."

"But you were secretive…"

"And what law is there against wanting privacy, huh? Maybe there's a rule in Blithedale that everyone's life needs to be put under a microscope, but I don't live in Blithedale. I'm a private person and I choose to keep to myself, which people can't accept. They're always blaming people like me for being 'unsociable' or even 'sneaky.'"

Alice winced. She'd been guilty of suspecting Nelson because he was aloof. But he was right: people had the right to keep to themselves without being branded 'strange'—or worse yet, a killer.

"So what happened with Cliff?"

"Cliff came to see me. He threatened me, insisting that I'd been jealous and wanted Sasha to myself." Nelson shook his head. "I loved Sasha. She was my only real friend here. But jealous? I'm not the jealous type."

Alice said, "And that convinced Cliff?"

"No. He wanted proof. But how do you prove that you're not the kind of person who would kill someone because they're a jealous maniac? I could take a polygraph test or swear on the Bible, but that wasn't going to convince him, either."

"So how did you convince him?"

"I proved I'd never date Sasha. I'm gay. I told Cliff that. In Cliff's mind, that cleared everything up. He's convinced Sasha's murder has to be about jealousy, and as soon as I made it clear that I wasn't romantically interested in his girl-friend, he wrote me off. As if gay men can't be jealous killers. We can be anything—and anyone—imaginable." Nelson quirked a smile. "So, yeah, by pigeon-holing me, he let me off the hook. Yay for stereotypes."

Alice nodded. Nelson captured Cliff's logic so well, and it made sense that in the grieving boyfriend's mind, the killer had to be a rival. She wondered why he hadn't suspected Silas. But who knew what would happen if he changed his mind about Fran—maybe he'd set his sights on the conserva-tionist instead, suddenly convinced he was the killer.

Nelson said, "Look, Cliff can be a goon. But he's also deeply wounded. I decided to give him some leeway. After all, he and I have something in common: we both saw what an amazing person Sasha was. I mean, she was willing to give up everything for the Blithedale Woods, donating all her extra income to the conservation society."

"She was devoted," Alice said, nodding.

"And so hopeful about what they could achieve," Nelson continued. "That night at the Woodlander Bar, Sasha was giddy with excitement—she felt the universe was preparing to help her win the lottery so she could help save the Blithedale Woods. When she bought her lottery ticket, she pulled one with her lucky number. She saw it as an omen."

"What was her lucky number?"

Nelson shrugged. "If she told me, I can't remember. Just that it was a lucky number, and that it was close to her heart."

As Alice thanked Nelson for his honesty, her phone rang.

"Captain," she said, answering Captain Burlap's call.

He cut straight to the chase. "Alice, we've looked for Fran at her home and we've asked her employees. No one's seen her."

A sickening dread roiled Alice's insides. Cliff was out for revenge, and there was no telling what he might do. Could he have taken Fran? And if so, what was he planning to do?

Burlap said, "I'm heading to Opal's home to talk to her. Want to join me?"

CHAPTER 26

"Can you tell us about Fran?" Captain Burlap said, almost yelling over the sound of the TV.

Opal's mom sat on a couch that sagged almost as much as she did. She stared dull-eyed at a game show on the TV, its volume cranked to ear-deafening levels. Her hands rested in a bowl of popcorn on her lap. She didn't move. She hadn't even glanced at the visitors, as if nothing could distract her from the flickering screen.

Opal motioned for Alice and Burlap to follow her.

The modest ranch-style home—similar to others Alice had been inside before—was littered with piles of magazines, discarded shopping bags, and dirty laundry. As Opal led them into her bedroom, Alice glanced through a doorway to the kitchen. The sink overflowed with food-crusted pots and plates and cups. A pizza box lay on the kitchen table, its top yawning open to reveal grease stains on the cardboard, and nothing else.

In her bedroom, Opal shut the door behind them and sat cross-legged on her bed. She didn't offer Alice and Burlap a seat. Posters on the walls showed celebrities and other attractive people with beautiful hair. There was a desk with a ring light, a mirror, and a jumble of makeup.

"You live here with your mom?" Burlap asked.

Opal, arms crossed, said, "Yeah, so what?"

"Just confirming the facts. How about you tell me about Fran?"

"What's to tell? Fran and I had a fight at work and I left. I needed some space. She's, like, all up in my face all the time, and it drives me crazy."

"Did you go back?"

Opal shook her head. "No. But I called to tell Fran I wouldn't be coming in this afternoon. I wasn't feeling well."

"And what did Fran say?"

"Nothing. She didn't answer. I called the salon. I called her cell. No answer."

Alice and Burlap exchanged glances.

Alice said, "Do you know Cliff, Sasha's boyfriend?"

"Not really. I mean, I've met him. He liked one of my posts on social. But it's not like he commented or anything."

"Any idea where he might be?"

Opal shook her head.

Alice tried another tack. "How did Fran feel about Sasha?"

Opal shrugged. "How should I know?"

Alice sat down on the bed, perching on the edge. Closer to Opal now, she lowered her voice to appear more intimate, more confidential. "How did you feel about Sasha?"

"Sasha was Sasha."

"She was popular."

Opal had been frowning, and now the crease between her brows deepened.

"I guess," she said.

"Did it bother you that Sasha was Candy's star stylist?"

"What do I care?"

Opal looked away, her voice going for disinterest, but her body language betraying her. Alice had struck a nerve.

"You put a lot into your personal brand," she said. "It must be tough to put so much work into something and yet feel that others aren't noticing."

Opal turned back to her, eyeing her suspiciously. "I guess…"

Alice added, "And it's especially tough if popularity comes easy for other people."

Opal nodded. "You mean Sasha."

She spoke Sasha's name with real venom, then said, "Even now, she's getting more attention on social media than I am. Everyone's like, 'Oh, poor Sasha,' and I'm like, 'Hello, I'm here too.'"

"That must be so frustrating," Alice said, suppressing her own disgust at Opal's incredible selfishness. She spoke softly, trying to show that she was sympathetic to Opal. Behind her, she sensed Burlap's big, calm presence. She said, "Now I can see why Sasha's popularity must've been extra frustrating. But I actually thought you were friends. I mean, you took selfies together."

"Sasha wasn't my friend," Opal spat. "But every time I took a photo with her, I got more likes, so I kept doing it." She studied her fingers, tugging at a cuticle, then sighed deeply. "Even now, when I repost our photos together and share something about my grief, I get more likes than on any other post."

"So you do feel sad about Sasha dying?"

"Nah, it's just what you say on social."

Alice looked at Burlap, who shook his head, no doubt in despair over Opal's attitude, as well as at the lack of information about where Fran and Cliff might be. Getting anything out of Opal would be pointless.

Alice got to her feet.

"Call me if you hear anything," Burlap said, handing Opal his card.

Outside the house, Alice took a deep breath of fresh air, relieved to have escaped. There was an oppressive atmosphere in that home.

"The air is bad in there," she said.

"It's not just the air," Burlap said.

Neither commented more on Opal and her opinions. Alice knew Burlap shared her outrage. Grief was "just a thing." Sympathy was a pose to get more comments and likes on social media. Alice took another deep breath, eager to clear her lungs of the stale air from inside Opal's home.

She considered Opal's obsession with social media, and how she was constantly taking selfies, even of colleagues she didn't like. She wondered about the ones with Sasha. Digging out her phone, she found one of Opal's social media profiles.

She scrolled through the endless ream of photos. Recent posts included photos of Sasha, with expressions of sympathy and grief from Opal. There was even a video in which Opal appeared to be crying over her "friend's tragic death."

"Can you believe it?" she said, showing Burlap the posts.

He tsk-tsked and shook his head.

Alice kept scrolling until she found the older photos. There were photos of Opal, Candy, and Sasha at the salon, one with the three of them holding up their lottery tickets with the numbers 7017, 1313, and 7071, and another of Opal handing Sasha a mochaccino, the caption saying, "I'm such a giver. It makes me feel SO good. I made this drink for my work bestie, Sasha. She can't resist my mochaccino! #Work-Friends."

A more recent photo showed Opal and Fran together, with Opal handing Fran a mochaccino. The caption was almost identical. Apparently, Opal wasn't above recycling ideas.

Alice lowered her phone. "This gets us no closer to finding Fran."

Burlap nodded. "State troopers are searching Cliff's apartment in Tilbury Town. I'll join them. Maybe we can find a clue that will lead us to him. Need a ride back to town?"

Alice got into Burlap's cruiser. As they pulled out of the little driveway, she glanced back at the house and caught Opal staring out of her bedroom window at them. Then Opal raised her phone and snapped a photo of them.

Alice sighed. Even a visit from a cop was potential content for social media.

CHAPTER 27

"How's the investigation?" Becca asked as she leaned across the diner counter to refill Alice's cup.

Alice, sitting on a stool, nursed her third cup of coffee. Becca's question made her grimace.

"That bad, huh?" Becca said.

"Honestly? My brain tells me we're far from the truth, but my gut says we're close. But I can't figure out why."

"Like your subconscious is telling you something?"

"Yeah, but what?"

Becca smiled. "You'll figure it out, Alice. You always do."

A customer called for the check and Becca headed off to his table. Watching Becca walk away, Alice shook her head. She wasn't so sure. Her ideas about Sasha's death were a jumble of facts and suspicions, and far too rough around the edges to lead her to anything concrete.

If she had more time, this would be fine. But she didn't. Fran was missing. Cliff had abducted her. And if it hadn't been for her own meddling, it would never have happened.

Captain Burlap said they'd pulled security footage from a business on Main Street that showed Cliff driving off with Fran on the back of his motorbike. She didn't look tied-up, but that didn't mean he hadn't threatened her—or somehow coerced her. Maybe Cliff had a gun.

"Penny for your thoughts?"

Ona put a hand on her shoulder. Alice moved her jacket, which was lying on the stool next to hers, and Ona sat down and ordered a coffee. Becca returned to the other side of the counter and filled a cup for Ona. Bundling up her jacket, Alice felt a lump inside. That would be her copy of *Walden*, still nestled inside the inner pocket.

She sighed. *Imagine a quiet day, sitting in Wonderland Books, sipping a cup of mint tea and reading* Walden. *Oh, wouldn't that be nice.*

But instead she had a killer to catch, and a crazy widowed boyfriend on the rampage.

Together, they reviewed the case so far, going over the details: the burglary at the hair salon, Sasha's death by poisoning, and the suspects—from Cliff to Silas, and from Fran to Opal. They talked through Fran's situation, and how unhappy she seemed to be with her new salon, as well as Opal's social media obsession, her selfies, and how much she'd disliked Sasha.

As they talked, Alice heard laughter and looked up. In a booth near the back, Candy was drinking coffee and eating cake with a few other regulars: Lorraine, the public librarian, and her best friend, Sandy. In the booth next to them, Silas was entertaining a young woman, no doubt a volunteer at the conservation society, and he was talking at her as she nodded earnestly, her chin resting on her hands as she gazed admiringly at him. He said something, and she burst out laughing and reached across the table to touch his hand.

Irritation prickled Alice's skin. She was tempted to walk over and tell the girl to watch out—Silas wasn't worth worshipping. Besides, he might have something to do with this murder.

She turned back to Becca and Ona. "I feel the truth is staring us right in the face."

"It often is," Ona said.

"From what you say,"—Becca leaned close to Alice and Ona—"Opal sounds very suspicious."

Alice said, "But does that make her a killer? Still, there is something about those selfies she took…"

"The ones where she made mochaccinos for Sasha?" Ona asked. "Or when she and Candy and Sasha bought lottery tickets?"

"Did someone say my name?" Candy approached them. "Something about some photos?"

"Oh, we're just talking about the murder investigation," Becca said, "and some selfies Opal took of you and Sasha buying lottery tickets."

"Actually, I was thinking of the photo with the mochaccino," Alice said.

Candy made a face. "Awful stuff. I never touched it. Give me real coffee any day of the week. In fact, I came to get another coffee. And to ask about poor Fran. Any news?"

Becca shook her head as she refilled Candy's cup. "No word on her disappearance yet."

Candy put a hand to her heart, her eyebrows creasing with concern. "Let me know if you hear anything. I'll be up all night worrying about her."

At that moment, Alice's phone buzzed and lit up. It was Captain Burlap calling.

He said, "I found Fran."

"Is she alive? And what about Cliff?"

"I believe Cliff's holding her hostage. But at least she's alive."

"Thank goodness."

"Alice?" Burlap drew in a breath. "Cliff wants to talk. But he insists on seeing you, and no one else."

CHAPTER 28

The trees formed a dense obstacle course in front of Sasha's tiny house. Captain Burlap moved from tree trunk to tree trunk, guiding Alice closer and closer until there was only open ground between them and the front door.

"I've called for backup," he said. "We should wait."

"Wait for Fran to get hurt?" Alice shook her head. "I'm going in."

"Don't be a hero."

"Listen, Cliff served me tea in that tiny house. I doubt he's suddenly going to clobber me over the head with the teapot."

She left the safety of the trees. Twigs snapped under her feet. Then, moving onto firmer ground, gravel crunched. It shifted beneath her feet. Heck, the whole world seemed to shift beneath her feet. Even if she'd convinced Captain Burlap that Cliff wasn't so dangerous, she wasn't sure she'd convinced herself.

She passed Cliff's motorbike.

She was five paces from the front door with its carved

wooden heart when the door cracked open and Cliff, still unseen, called out.

"Stop."

She stopped.

"You aren't armed, are you?"

Alice raised her arms. "Of course not."

"What's that bulge in your jacket?"

She patted her pocket, realizing what she was still carrying around.

"My copy of *Walden*."

"*Walden?*"

"You know, Thoreau. *Walden*. 'I went to the woods because I wished to live deliberately…'"

"Oh."

Long silence from behind the door. Then, finally, Cliff said, "All right. Come inside. I guess it's safe."

At the door, she reached out to pull it open. It swung open and a gigantic hand emerged to grasp her wrist. She let out a gasp as Cliff hauled her inside, sending her stumbling across the floor and slamming into the kitchen table. Behind her, he shut the door.

With her hands on the table, she looked over her shoulder at him. He was holding what looked like a weapon in one hand. A gun?

His eyebrows bunched up. "Are you OK?"

She straightened up and rubbed her right arm, which felt bruised after the collision with the table.

"Sorry." Cliff scratched the back of his neck, looking embarrassed. "Sometimes I get carried away."

Facing him, Alice now saw what he was holding. It wasn't a gun. It was a gas lighter, one of those long-snouted things that helped you fire up a stove or a grill without burning your fingers.

He looked down at the object in his hand. "Uh," he said.

"It's not what you think...I was about to make a pot of tea. You want some?"

"Cliff," Alice said. "What have you gotten yourself into?"

"I—" His face fell. "I don't know. After insisting Fran come with me, we drove around for a while. Then I brought her here. I didn't know where else to go."

She looked around. "Where's Fran?"

"She's in the bedroom."

Alice made a move toward the door, then stopped herself, aware that Cliff might be jumpy. "Do you mind if I check on her?"

"Uh, sure. I'll make some tea."

Alice opened the door to the tiny bedroom. The curtains were closed. It was dim inside, but not so dim that Alice couldn't see.

Fran lay on the bed, propped up with a dozen pillows. She looked up from reading a book.

"Oh, hi, Alice," she said with a sigh. "What a mess, huh?"

"Are you all right? Did Cliff hurt you?"

Her eyes widened. "Hurt me? Why would he do that? The guy's confused. Started jabbering about how I might've poisoned Sasha, and he said I needed to come with him. I said fine. Honestly, I was relieved to be kidnapped, if that's what this is." She let out a long sigh. "I can't remember the last time I got to sit in a quiet, dark bedroom. Or when I got to read a book."

She turned the book over, revealing the cover. It was Ursula LeGuin's *A Wizard of Earthsea*.

"One of my favorite books," she explained.

Alice gaped at her. Fran seemed calmer than she'd ever seen her. She certainly didn't look like your textbook example of a kidnapping victim.

Turning back into the main room, she confronted Cliff.

"What in the world were you thinking?"

Cliff sheepishly looked down at the pot of tea he held. He'd set out cups on a coffee table by the sofa and armchair. "Tea? I've got some cookies here somewhere, too."

He didn't wait for her to answer, but poured a steaming cup for her.

She took the cup and watched him pour one for himself, then prepared a cup for Fran, carrying it into the bedroom for her. Alice heard Fran say, "Thanks, Cliff, you're a sweetheart."

Cliff returned to the living room and sat down. He sipped his tea. Then he dropped his voice to a whisper. "I want to know something…"

"You want to know something? You're not the only one."

He put a finger to his mouth and gestured toward the bedroom.

"Fran didn't kill Sasha, did she?" he whispered.

"Well, what do you think?"

Cliff looked down at his tea.

"I was convinced when I confronted her," he muttered. "But now, not so much…"

From the other room, Fran called out, "Not so much? You know I didn't do it, you oaf."

Cliff winced. "But she broke into the salon…"

Alice turned to look at Fran through the doorway.

Fran grimaced. "Well, that much is true. I still have my old key and I know the alarm, so I snuck in. I broke into the salon to borrow a blow dryer, some scissors, combs, and other gear. I didn't have enough on hand. My supplier didn't deliver everything I'd ordered. So I borrowed some stuff. I was going to bring it all back—I swear."

Alice recalled Sasha accusing Opal of taking her blow dryer. Fran had taken it.

"What about the mochaccino mix?"

"It was on the shelf by Opal's chair. But I didn't touch it. Why would I? I have my own."

"When Ona and I showed up, you took off on your Vespa."

"I felt guilty borrowing stuff from Candy's salon. When you saw me, I panicked and ran."

Alice considered this information. She didn't doubt Fran was telling the truth. That meant the burglar wasn't the killer. Someone else had spiked the mochaccino mix before Sasha drank the coffee. But who else had access?

A thought flitted down in the depths of her mind. The flash of insight flared, then disappeared again into the dark.

"The answer's staring me in the face," she mumbled. "I know it…"

She frowned and stared into the middle distance, trying to grasp the elusive clue that would tie it all together.

Outside, Captain Burlap yelled, "Hey, Alice, are you all right? Cliff, let her show herself to prove she's OK."

Cliff gave her a nod, and she went to the front door, opening it a crack, so she could stick her head out and wave at Burlap. Across the distance, Burlap raised a hand, giving her a thumbs up. Behind her, Cliff appeared in the doorway and called out: "Captain Burlap, uh…would you like some tea and cookies?"

Alice was about to close the door when her eyes fell on the carved heart with the house number.

Wait a second…

She closed the door and brought out her phone.

"Opal's selfies…"

She found Opal's social media profile, suddenly certain that she knew how to find the answer. She scrolled through the feed. But where were the selfies Opal had posted with her colleagues? They were gone. Deleted.

As she refreshed the feed, another selfie—one with Opal and Sasha—vanished.

An icy chill ran down her spine.

Then, right in front of her eyes, another disappeared.

The cold spread through her limbs.

I can't believe it...it can't be true...

But it was true: someone was deleting the photos, one by one.

The killer was erasing the evidence.

CHAPTER 29

Alice jumped into the police cruiser. Captain Burlap turned on his siren and slammed his foot down on the accelerator. The car flew through the woods. Alice clung to her seat, the bumps tossing her back and forth. Her teeth banged against each other so hard she feared that, after this emergency was over, she'd need dental work.

Finally, the dirt road spat them out of the backwoods and they hit smooth blacktop. Burlap threw the steering wheel to the side and pulled the cruiser into another turn in the road, expertly keeping them from careening into the trees.

"I get the feeling you've done this before," she said.

"Yup." Then he added, "Still no luck reaching Opal?"

Alice dialed the number again, then shook her head when she got voicemail again. "No. She's not answering."

Both of them knew what it must mean. But they weren't sure what their final destination would be, so they headed for the nearest one first. Burlap steered the cruiser down a familiar residential street. With a screech, they came to a standstill by Opal's home. In an instant, they were both out of the car and bounding up to the entrance. Burlap hammered on the door. It didn't take long before it opened and Opal's mom stared wide-eyed at them. She clutched a pillow against her chest.

"Opal," she said, her lower lip quivering. "Something's wrong. She won't answer her phone."

"We know. Any idea where she might be?"

The woman shook her head. "When she isn't here, she's at work. I can't think of where else she'd be."

Alice and Burlap exchanged looks. Alice said, "Then you're right: she's at work."

Digging out her phone, Alice sent a quick text to Becca and Ona:

Emergency. Keep an eye on Candy's salon. But don't go in. Meet you there.

Five minutes later, they sat in Burlap's cruiser outside Candy's Hair Salon. The blinds were down, the place apparently closed.

As Alice got out of the cruiser, Becca and Ona came running up.

Ona said, "As soon as you texted, we checked out the salon. The blinds are down. The sign says they're closed. But it's early—and frankly strange—for Candy to close for the day."

Burlap pulled his gun. "I'm going in."

Alice said, "Wait. Let me try this first."

She stepped up to the door, then gestured for the others to get out of sight. Burlap stepped behind his cruiser. After hesitating, so did Becca and Ona. Then Alice knocked on the door. Her knock, firm and loud, would sound all the way to the back of the salon.

A minute later, the blinds shook and parted. A pair of tired eyes looked out and came to rest on Alice. Candy blinked. Then the blinds closed again, and the door clicked open.

Candy peered out at Alice. "Hi, Alice. We're closed, but if you need to book an appointment, let's talk tomorrow."

"I'm looking for Opal."

"Why?" Candy said, a little too quickly. "I haven't seen her."

"See, she sent me a long message with a bunch of photos. Oddly, they're selfies of her, you, and Sasha."

Candy's eyes widened. "Oh." She opened the door a little more. "You'd better come inside."

Alice stepped through the door, and as soon as she was inside the salon, Candy shut it behind her. She turned the lock with a loud click.

Alice looked around for signs of Opal. The back door to the break room was closed. On the shelf by Opal's mirror lay a cell phone. No doubt hers.

Candy stepped past Alice to the mirror, and Alice was sure the salon owner was going to grab the phone. And she did reach down and grab an object from the shelf, but when she turned around, it wasn't the phone she was holding.

It was a barber razor, its blade dangerously sharp.

"You shouldn't have meddled, Alice."

Candy's hand shook. But her face, though haggard with fatigue, looked rock hard with determination.

"I just want to make sure Opal is all right," Alice said.

"She's all right. Knocked out and tied up, but all right. I lured her here with a promise of more money. Then I drugged her."

Alice nodded. "And then you deleted the photos, trying to get rid of the incriminating evidence."

The razor shook even more. "I can't risk anyone guessing what happened. Not when I'm so close…"

"So close to what?"

"To saving my salon."

"You killed Sasha, so you could steal her winning lottery ticket, didn't you?"

Candy glared. "Sasha was going to throw it away on Silas's little pet project. Oh, I like the woods as much as anyone. But what about me? Everyone wants to save the trees, but what about my salon? Candy's Hair Salon has been a staple of Blithedale for more than 20 years. Why is that less important than a forest?"

Alice said, "You swapped your ticket for Sasha's."

"Seven, zero, one, seven," Candy said. "That was her number. My number—7071—was so similar. But 17 was her lucky number. What an odd lucky number."

"It was the number on her tiny house, the home she loved."

Candy grimaced. "Because of the break-in, I was at the salon with the police when the winning number was announced. Sasha had left her ticket on her shelf. I swapped it for mine. But I knew that eventually she'd realize someone took her ticket. All she had to do was check Opal's stupid selfie. It proved it."

"So you spiked the mochaccino mix to kill Sasha. But why didn't you get rid of Opal's selfies earlier?"

"Opal left me. I tried to lure her back, so I could steal her phone, even for just a moment. But that girl is glued to her phone. It's more important to her than the salon. I'm the only one who seems to value this salon…"

She stared down at the floor, frowning. Then, looking up again and focusing on Alice, she raised the razor again.

"Opal's selfies are gone, deleted. Now I want those photos on your phone. Hand 'em over."

Alice said nothing. She stood perfectly still.

Candy eyed her suspiciously, then said, "You don't have the photos, do you? You never did. You lied." She ran a hand across her forehead, as if she were sweating. The other still held the razor. "I need you and Opal to keep your mouths shut."

She took a step toward Alice. The razor shook a little less now.

Alice backed away. She said, "You deleted the photos off social media. But did you remember to delete them from Opal's own photo app?"

"Of course. I'm not a complete fool."

"But did you clear the trash folder? Otherwise, it stays in there for weeks."

Candy's face went rigid. She turned to look at Opal's phone on the counter behind her. Now, while Candy was momentarily distracted, Alice could act. But she had no weapon. She reached for the only thing she could find on her person—the book in her jacket's inner pocket.

Candy must've heard her jacket rustle, because she whipped around again and thrust out the blade.

Alice whipped out the copy of *Walden*, thrusting it upward, catching the razor. It sliced into the paperback, deep into the meat of Thoreau's book. Candy struggled to withdraw her blade. It was stuck.

Alice grabbed Candy's wrist and twisted it.

"Aaaah," Candy cried out, a mixture of surprise and anger and pain.

Behind Alice, the door crashed open as Captain Burlap came charging in. But Becca and Ona, barreling past him, reached Candy first, throwing themselves at her and knocking her over. There was a clatter and a bang as the three went down, overturning chairs and carts with salon equipment. In an instant, they had Candy pinned to the ground.

"We got her," Ona said.

Alice clutched her copy of *Walden* in front of her, the barber's razor still stuck in the middle.

Burlap, holstering his gun, eyed the book. He said, "Who knew Thoreau could be such a lifesaver?"

"And the moral is," Alice said, "never leave home without a book."

CHAPTER 30

*T*hat Saturday, Alice hosted a "Walden Party" at Wonderland Books. She'd devoted an entire display to *Walden* and books related to it, from *Henry David Thoreau: A Life* by Laura Dassow Walls to *Pilgrim at Tinker Creek* by Annie Dillard—all of them discounted in celebration of the classic, and its unconventional role in protecting Alice. On a little placard by the stack of *Walden* paperbacks, Alice had written, "This book may save your life."

The owner of the local art shop, Dorian, had painted a series of watercolors of Walden Pond, Thoreau sitting outside his cabin, and one of Alice holding a book with a razor blade stuck in its cover. They dangled from strings that stretched across the tiny house bookstore. Becca provided coffee, tea, and juice, courtesy of the What the Dickens Diner, while Andrea from Bonsai & Pie dished out her famous apple crumble.

People thronged the bookstore. An atmosphere of celebration pervaded the party, and Alice had no illusions that it was all thanks to her sale on *Walden*.

Blithedale was celebrating other good news, too.

Silas, standing next to her with a cup of coffee, was telling her all about the conservation society's success. They had won battles on two fronts. First, the development firm responsible for the construction on Main Street had redrawn the lot, no longer building on forest land. And second, the town council had voted almost unanimously—with only the mayor against—to change the rules to allow tiny houses within Blithedale, both for homes and for businesses.

"And then there's the lottery prize money," Alice added.

Silas raised his eyebrows. "The lottery? But Candy won that."

"Candy stole it. Sasha should rightfully have claimed the prize, and everyone knew her intention was to donate it to the conservation society. Once we clear up the legal details, the Blithedale Future Fund will release the money to your organization."

Silas grabbed Alice's free hand—she held a cup of coffee in the other—and pumped it. "Thank you, thank you."

Alice smiled.

He walked off to tell Fran the news about the lottery. Fran stood at the other end of the room talking to Beau, Lorraine, and Sandy. Alice watched Silas interrupt them, so he could share his good news. With emphasis on *his*. She shook her head. Silas had done incredible work to protect the Blithedale Woods, but that didn't change how she felt about his big ego.

As she watched, Fran cut off Silas in mid-sentence and broke away from the group, excusing herself to the others. Silas blinked, clearly surprised that one of his devoted followers would walk away from him.

When Fran reached Alice, she smiled.

Alice cocked her head, studying Fran. "You look different somehow."

Fran laughed. "I didn't change my hairstyle, if that's what you mean."

No, she didn't. But she laughed and her eyes sparkled with something Alice hadn't seen before: vitality, joy, and freedom. The fatigue and stress that had burdened her seemed to have lifted.

Fran said, "Didn't I tell you? I'm closing the salon and downsizing. I was never happy as a people manager or salon owner. I want to cut and style hair, and make my customers happy, but I can do that better by keeping things small."

"Tiny, in fact," Ona said, coming toward them. "Sorry I'm late, Alice."

"Hard at work?" Alice said, eyeing the sawdust that covered Ona's clothes.

"In fact, hard at work on Fran's new tiny house."

Fran's face broke into a big smile. "I can't wait to see it. I'm going to open my own one-person salon in a tiny house."

"And now that the zoning regulations have changed," Ona said, "you can put your tiny house anywhere in Blithedale, including on Main Street." She ran a hand across her forehead, smearing sawdust, dirt, and sweat together. "Phew. Suddenly, my tiny house business is skyrocketing. I've never been so busy. I've got people calling from across the state—they heard about the conservation society's success from *The Blithedale Record* or even national news, and they're interested in what they call 'sustainable living' in Blithedale."

Fran nodded. "Just in the past 24 hours, Blithedale has appeared on websites for tiny house enthusiasts and even on lists of 'best places to live close to nature' and that kind of thing. We're moving up in the world."

"The inn is getting more reservations than ever," Ona said, and then grinned. "I can hardly keep up."

Alice said, "After I close today, I'll come help at the inn—or with building your tiny houses."

"Or both," Ona said.

"Or both," Alice agreed with a smile. It filled her with joy to see Ona so giddy with excitement and suddenly so successful. With the new town council regulations, it seemed as if Blithedale had turned a corner—a brighter, even more interesting future lay ahead.

Becca joined them, handing Ona a cup of coffee. As if reading Alice's thoughts, she said, "This town is poised for a lot of changes ahead. Positive change. I can feel it in my bones."

"And you can read it in *The Blithedale Record*," Todd said from nearby.

They all laughed.

As they drank their coffee, someone cleared their throat to draw their attention. Alice glanced over and saw Mayor MacDonald. Usually, he strode into her bookstore with his characteristic dramatic flair. But although he still wore his Mark Twain suit, he'd moved into the store quietly, and when he spoke, he stumbled over the words, his face flushing with embarrassment.

"Ona," he said. "Do you have 5 minutes to talk?"

"Me?" Ona said. "You want to talk to me?"

"If you have time…" He grimaced, visibly awkward at his own apologetic tone. "See, I have several clients who are enquiring about properties in the area, but they're only interested if…" He drew in a sharp breath and frowned. "Only if they can build tiny houses."

"Oh." Ona's one visible eyebrow rose sharply. Then sunk as she quirked a wry smile. "Oh, of course. I'll be happy to help, mayor. Why don't we go over to the inn and talk business?"

"Wonderful," the mayor muttered. "Thank you."

Ona winked at Alice and Becca before putting a hand on the mayor's back and guiding him out of the bookstore.

Alice said, "That's the first time I've heard the mayor use the words 'thank you'—what's next? 'I'm sorry'?"

Becca chuckled. "Don't hold your breath."

They were joking, and yet Alice really was amazed at how diminished the recent ordeal had left Mayor MacDonald. Once again, she wondered how long he'd last in his job.

Becca must've been thinking along the same lines, because she said, "Good thing Mayor MacDonald's realty business is doing well, because I don't think his career in politics will last much longer."

"People are ready for a change," Alice said.

Becca nodded. "I've heard rumors that Silas plans to run against MacDonald in the upcoming election."

"I heard that, too. But my gut tells me Blithedale is ready for real change. The men with big egos have had their time. The next mayor will be different."

Becca raised an eyebrow. "You know, that's what I was thinking, too."

Neither said any more. They sipped their coffees, standing close together, and Alice was sure she knew what Becca was thinking of: Blithedale's next mayor. And, in her own mind, there was only one ideal candidate.

Again, Becca's thoughts matched her own. She said, "She'll need help if she's going to win."

"Well, then," Alice said, taking a sip of coffee, "we'll just have to help her, won't we?"

Becca grinned. "Yes, we will."

* * *

Thank you so much for visiting Blithedale.
Want a free short story? Sign up for my newsletter to hear when the next Wonderland Books

Cozy Mystery comes out and I'll send the free cozy mystery story to you by email:

https://mpblackbooks.com/newsletter/

Finally, if you enjoyed this book, please take a moment to leave a review online. It makes it easier for other readers to find the book. Thanks so much!

Turn the page to see what other books are available.

MORE BY M.P. BLACK

A Wonderland Books Cozy Mystery Series

A Bookshop to Die For

A Theater to Die For

A Halloween to Die For

A Christmas to Die For

A Yarn Shop to Die For

An Italian-American Cozy Mystery Series

The Soggy Cannoli Murder

Sambuca, Secrets, and Murder

Tastes Like Murder

Meatballs, Mafia, and Murder

Short stories

The Italian Cream Cake Murder (FREE)

ABOUT THE AUTHOR

M.P. Black writes fun cozies with an emphasis on food, books, and travel—and, of course, a good old murder mystery.

Besides writing and publishing his own books, he helps others fulfill their author dreams too through courses and coaching.

M.P. Black has lived in many places, including Brooklyn, Vienna, and San Jose de Costa Rica. Today, he and his family live in Copenhagen, Denmark, where coziness ("hygge") is a national pastime.

Join M.P. Black's free newsletter for updates on books and special deals:

https://mpblackbooks.com/newsletter/

Made in the USA
Columbia, SC
03 August 2024